He lived

Not like other people. He no longer had a Social Security number, no service record, no contacts beyond his immediate supervisor and occasional teammates. He didn't even have a pair of damn dog tags. Nothing that could identify him.

Alex was part of a shadow created by the U.S. government to deal with problems that could not be handled in open daylight. And when the shadow fell on the people who created those problems, they disappeared.

That was what he was trained for, what he was good at. Not trying to act normal, playing house with a senator's daughter. All he had to do was keep Nicola Barrington from getting too far under his skin in the next couple of days. Shouldn't take more than that for the rest of his team to pick up the shooter. Damn. He wasn't used to playing bodyguard. He was more of a seek-and-destroy man.

But guard her he would—at *any* cost.

Dear Harlequin Intrigue Reader,

To mark a month of fall festivals, screeching goblins and hot apple cider, Harlequin Intrigue has a provocative October lineup guaranteed to spice things up!

Debra Webb launches her brand-new spin-off series, COLBY AGENCY: INTERNAL AFFAIRS, with *Situation: Out of Control.* This first installment sets the stage for the most crucial mission of all…smoking out a mole in their midst. The adrenaline keeps flowing in *Rules of Engagement* by acclaimed author Gayle Wilson, who continues her PHOENIX BROTHERHOOD series with a gripping murder mystery that hurls an unlikely couple into a vortex of danger.

Also this month, a strictly business arrangement turns into a lethal attraction, in *Cowboy Accomplice* by B.J. Daniels—book #2 in her Western series, McCALLS' MONTANA. And just in time for Halloween, October's haunting ECLIPSE selection, *The Legacy of Croft Castle* by Jean Barrett, promises to put you in that spooky frame of mind.

There are more thrills to come when Kara Lennox unveils the next story in her CODE OF THE COBRA series, with *Bounty Hunter Redemption,* which pits an alpha male lawman against a sexy parole officer when mayhem strikes. And, finally this month, watch for the action-packed political thriller *Shadow Soldier* by talented newcomer Dana Marton. This debut book spotlights an antiterrorist operative who embarks on a high-stakes mission to dismantle a diabolical ticking time bomb.

Enjoy!

Denise O'Sullivan
Senior Editor
Harlequin Intrigue

SHADOW SOLDIER

DANA MARTON

HARLEQUIN®

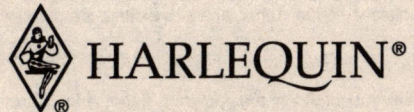

TORONTO • NEW YORK • LONDON
AMSTERDAM • PARIS • SYDNEY • HAMBURG
STOCKHOLM • ATHENS • TOKYO • MILAN • MADRID
PRAGUE • WARSAW • BUDAPEST • AUCKLAND

ISBN 0-373-22806-6

SHADOW SOLDIER

This edition published by arrangement with Harlequin Books S.A.

www.eHarlequin.com

Printed in U.S.A.

ABOUT THE AUTHOR

Dana Marton lives near Wilmington, Delaware, and is married to her very own soldier hero. She has been an avid reader since childhood and has a master's degree in writing popular fiction. When not writing, she can be found either in her large garden or her home library.

She would love to hear from her readers via e-mail at DanaMarton@yahoo.com, or your can send post mail to: Dana Marton, P.O. Box 7987, Newark, DE 19714. SASE appreciated.

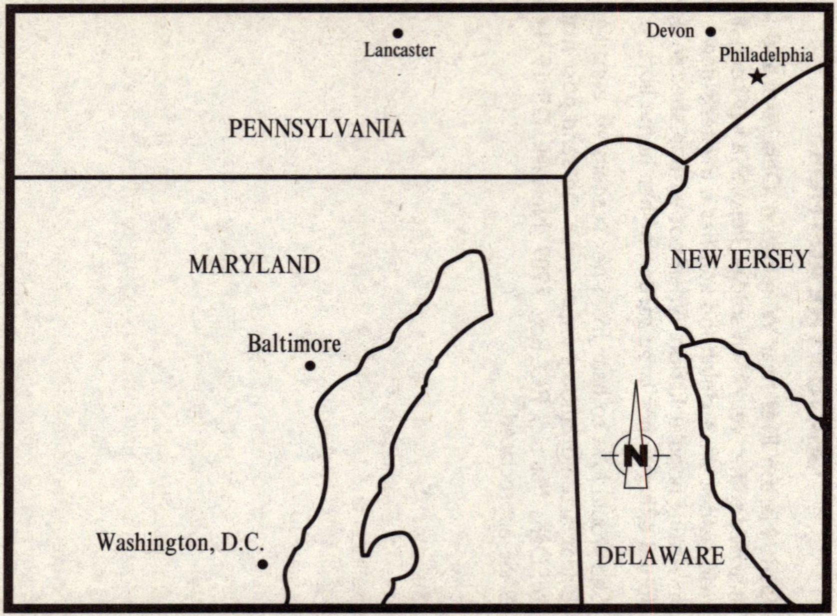
Lancaster
Devon
Philadelphia
PENNSYLVANIA
MARYLAND
NEW JERSEY
Baltimore
N
Washington, D.C.
DELAWARE

CAST OF CHARACTERS

Nicola Barrington—For years, Nicola has managed to stay out of the limelight that surrounded her high-profile father. But when terrorists attempt to kill her, she's pulled back into the world of political intrigue by the only man who can save her.

Alejandro (Alex) Jesús Rodriguez—Member of a top secret military group (Special Designation Defense Unit) established to fight terrorism. He does whatever it takes to protect his country, even breaking the rules when he has to. Except one—he never gets personally involved.

Senator Edward Barrington—Nicola's father, ex-U.S. Ambassador to China. He has many enemies, political and personal, and more than his fair share of secrets to hide.

General Meng—Once a top military man, he disappeared from a Chinese prison five years ago. Has he been killed, or is he hunting those he thinks betrayed him?

Du Shaozu—Nicola's latest client makes it clear he's interested in more than Nicola's consulting skills, but is romance what he really wants?

Spike—Alex's teammate. He came to the SDDU from the FBI's language program. One of the few men whom Alex trusts without reservation.

Colonel Wilson—Alex's boss. He's the leader of the SDDU, reporting straight to the Homeland Security Secretary.

In memory of Sheila Conway,
a true friend and wonderful writer.

Acknowledgments

With many thanks to Adél for her unwavering support. Also, my sincere gratitude and appreciation go to two wonderful writers, Jenel Looney and Anita Staley, for their endless patience and help, and to the faculty at Seton Hill University, especially Leslie Davis Guccione, mentor extraordinaire.

Chapter One

She moved like a symphony.

Her arms extended with elbows slightly bent and palms facing forward, she began by working each major muscle group, then guided her body through her regular poses, ending with her face upturned toward the rising sun.

Watching her practice Tai Chi every dawn turned bearable the job that made Alejandro Jesús Rodriguez want to jump out of his slowly recovering skin at least a dozen times a day. He focused on the balcony, on her upthrust breasts, as she glided into her next routine.

Unfortunately, as much as her curves eased his irritation at the assignment, they also brought their own set of frustrations. After two months of covert surveillance, every tantalizing detail of Nicola Barrington's body was etched into his mind to torment him whether or not he was looking. Her standard summer wear around the house—tank tops and ungodly short shorts—didn't help.

Alex swallowed as Nicola bent until her fingertips swept the floor, her mass of dark curls falling around her face, her incredible behind thrust toward the sky. He'd been put on around-the-clock duty a few hours after he'd gotten off the plane from Yemen. Having to watch Miss Barrington's mouthwatering figure 24/7 made his eyes pop several times a day—his eyes and a certain other body part.

He forced his gaze from the second-story balcony that extended from her bedroom and scanned the rest of the quarter-acre property along with as much of the street as he could see from his vantage point. No suspicious activity.

He had always hated this part of the job—the waiting. Eight weeks of sedate domestic duty was enough to drive him stir crazy even if it was supposed to be good for his recovery. He wanted action. Not that he wished any harm to the woman. He just wished the bad guys would make their move, already, so he could do his job. Or better yet, he wished Colonel Wilson would give the word that the transfer he had requested a few days ago had been approved, pull him off this detail and let him go back into the fray.

Of course, the Colonel might have invented the whole assignment to keep him out of trouble for a while. Alex wouldn't put it past the man. He wiped the sweat from his forehead. If he ever found out that was the case, he would strangle the overprotective SOB and consider it well worth the court-martial.

He rolled his neck to loosen the stiffening muscles and felt sweat run down his back as he sat on the floor cross-legged and watched. Nicola closed her eyes and pursed her generous lips as if she were humming to herself. Her movements flowed like an intricate dance. *Caliente abrasador.* Scorching hot. Both the weather and the woman. If he had to watch her much longer he might evaporate.

She took showers without pulling the shades.

Alex closed his eyes and swallowed a groan. She probably didn't know anyone could see in her second-story bathroom window. She had no idea an SDDU soldier had made her neighbor's kid's treehouse his nighttime surveillance headquarters. Neither did her neighbors. Aside from a select few, nobody in the world knew the SDDU existed. The Special Designation Defense Unit was America's latest secret weapon in the fight against terrorism.

He wanted to be in the fight, not in a damn treehouse in a suburb of Philadelphia.

Carefully manicured gardens, mature shade trees and well-kept houses with swimming pools were the features of Devon, a town on the fashionable Main Line. He had seen places like this on TV as a kid—never figured he would see one up close. He wouldn't have believed anyone back then who'd told him it would be under these circumstances.

His gaze followed Nicola as she finished her Tai Chi and moved inside her two-story Federal-style home to start the business part of her day. She spent most of her time either working on her computer or meeting clients, growing her consulting company, Barrington International Trade Services, Ltd. The most action he'd seen in the past two months had been following Nicola from office to office as she conducted her appointments. She wasn't going anywhere today, though, nothing but phone calls on her schedule. He made sure to check her calendar every night when he sneaked in to secure the premises.

The house needed all the help he could give it. He liked the quaint brick exterior, but not the quaint security. Lack of security was more like it—one could hardly count the single dead bolt on the front door. The sliding glass doors to the small flagstone patio were as good as an invitation, same as the internal door connecting the garage with the laundry room, armed with only a twist knob. The windows were even more hopeless, originals from about fifty years ago when he estimated the house must have been built.

Alex wiped his forehead again as a brown van drove by for the second time. Not from the neighborhood. He knew every car within a three-block radius and to what driveway it belonged. Even with his binoculars, he could only make out shapes through the tinted windows—two people, a driver and a passenger.

Probably nothing to worry about. Could be house hunters, checking out the property for sale at the end of the street. He pulled out his cell phone, punched in the license plate number and saved it. When he reported in at noon, he would ask the Colonel to have his secretary run it. Just in case.

The garage door opened. Nicola. Alex watched as she backed out of the driveway, then he swung out of the tree and made a dash for his SUV parked one street down. He settled into a comfortable two-car distance behind her by the time she reached Route 30, the local thoroughfare. The woman drove like a ninety-year-old. I Brake for Finches proclaimed the bumper sticker on her late model Bonneville and that about summed it up.

He turned on the air conditioner full blast. Eastern Pennsylvania in July was murder. A hundred degrees at least today and no breeze in that treehouse. Not that he wasn't used to heat, he'd spent more than enough time in the desert, but the humidity got to him. If the air became any thicker he could give up breathing and start to chew and swallow.

She turned left into the first shopping plaza, crowded with designer-dressed yuppies stopping off for their caffe lattes on their way to work. He backed into the far corner of the parking lot for a clear view of both the cars and the building and left the motor running. He didn't have to follow her, knew exactly where she'd be going—to the Devon Farmers' Market. Hell, he could probably predict with ninety-nine percent accuracy what she'd be buying. All of it organic.

It wasn't right—watching a woman grocery shop. One of the most highly skilled soldiers in the country, and this was what they used him for. His jaw clenched from frustration. Already anticipating the excuses, he unclipped his cell phone from his belt to check on the transfer. He couldn't imagine anything happening on this assignment. Ever. Nicola Barrington didn't live that kind of a life. He wanted off the job.

He caught sight of the brown van from the corner of his eye as he punched the last number. Nicola was almost at the market door. He slammed his foot on the gas. The van's window rolled down in slow motion. The glint of metal caught his eyes. *Madre de Dios,* they were going to mow her down where she stood.

Two things flashed through his mind simultaneously: she was going to die, and it was his fault. He should have seen them coming from a mile away. Would have, if he hadn't gotten so damn complacent, having a pity party in the car instead of paying attention. What the hell was wrong with him? Tires squealing, he pulled to a stop between her and the first spray of bullets, and threw open the passenger-side door.

She crouched on the pavement, her head pulled down, her arms protecting her face—probably in too much shock to do anything else. Did she even notice him?

"Get in!" he yelled as the store windows exploded behind her.

PROPELLED BY ADRENALINE and a healthy survival instinct, Nicola leaped forward in the gunshot-peppered air and dove into the waiting SUV. The driver reached over and slammed the door shut behind her as the car surged ahead. Head down in the plane-crash-emergency position, she didn't look up until they were out of the parking lot, racing down the back streets.

"Thank you," she said finally when she found her voice and could stop shaking enough to sit up and look at the driver. The familiar face eased her panic somewhat. She'd seen him at the gym. For the past two months, they'd been on the same workout schedule. She wondered if he'd even noticed her. She'd noticed him of course. Every woman in the place had. Even the grandmothers.

"You have to turn right at the next light for the police station." She was far from calm, but functioning.

He ignored her and drove straight through the intersection. Probably couldn't slow down in time to make the turn.

"That's fine. Just take the next right and we can loop back."

He turned left. On red.

Unease pooled on the bottom of her stomach. A flock of confused thoughts circled in her head, too fast for her to grab and articulate any. "Who are you?"

"Put on your seat belt. Did you get a chance to look at them?"

"Not really." She'd been thinking about her grocery list when she'd heard the first bullets and got down. She hadn't had time to look around. The only things she could remember were the silhouettes in the van's window. "I think they wore masks."

"Keep your head down." His deep voice was hard, his face tight with concentration, as in a fluid motion he reached over her with his well-muscled arm and pulled a gun from the glove compartment into his lap.

She congratulated herself for not peeing her pants on the spot, then ducked as she'd been told and peeked around from her awkward position. The car was suspiciously free of holes. Bulletproof? She'd been in enough of them, during another life as the sheltered daughter of a U.S. ambassador, but why did the guy from the gym have a bulletproof car? And who was shooting at him?

Who was shooting at *her?* He had only darted into the picture to supposedly save her—or was he doing something far more sinister? Her father was a senator now. She considered for a moment whether the man's appearance out of nowhere had been a coincidence or part of a well-orchestrated plot.

''Am I being kidnapped?'' She straightened again, determined not to follow any more of his instructions until she assured herself they were for her benefit.

He glanced at her, surprise flashing across his hard-set face, and swore. ''No. Damn it, Nicola, keep your head down.''

He knew her name.

She swallowed and sat on her shaking hands. No need to let him see how scared she was. He'd probably been stalking her at the gym. God, how stupid could she be? She had liked him, had even entertained some thoughts of walking up to him someday and maybe getting to know him better.

She glanced at the gun. Sinister-looking firearms had definitely not been part of her plan.

As a kid, during her father's ambassadorship in China, they'd lived under constant guard, and she had often daydreamed about what she would do if something like this happened. She had imagined rebels breaking through the embassy gates. Since she was the smallest person in the compound, only she could escape, crawling through vent holes to the roof. She would go for help and save the hostages inside. Then her father would have come to her in tears of happiness and gratitude to tell her how proud she made him.

So much for the childish fantasy. Her limbs numb with fear, it took all her willpower not to whimper.

The car swerved, and she hung on for dear life. She was only twenty-five. Too young to die. *Then do something about it,* her mother's voice said in her head. Her mother had been the strong one in the family. Strong enough even to stand up to her father. But she hadn't inherited much of her mother's character. Maybe if they had spent more time together, some of it would have rubbed off. But there hadn't been time. Breast cancer had ripped her mother out of her young life with ruthless efficiency.

What would her mother say if she could see her now? *Don't let him intimidate you,* the little voice spoke again, and it certainly sounded like her mother. Nobody had intimidated Lillian Barrington. Nicola looked at her kidnapper. ''Who are you?''

''I'm here to protect you.''

''Right. What's your name?''

"Alex," he said it in a way that discouraged further inquiry.

She took in his wide shoulders and well-built body, the scars on the back of his hand, the gun. "Where are we going?" she pushed.

He grabbed his cell phone, flipped it open and dialed. "We had an incident at the Devon Farmers' Market. Shooting. She's fine. Brown van, 1990 Ford Econoliner. New York plates." He glanced at his phone and punched a button then read off a plate number from the screen.

When did he have the time to get that?

"Still in pursuit, going north on Route 202. Got anything open?" He paused. "Will do."

"Who was that?" she asked as he hung up the phone.

"My boss."

"Where are you taking me?"

"To a safe house, once we lose the tail." He swerved to the left.

It sounded utterly ridiculous. He looked the opposite of safe. She considered opening the door and hurling herself onto the pavement.

The passenger side mirror blew out, and she slid further down in the seat.

"The main body is bulletproof but the rest isn't." He swerved again. "I'm going to have to pick up some speed to get rid of them. Don't want to give them a chance to shoot out the tires.''

He took a sharp turn and she slammed against the door, the seat belt cutting into her stomach.

He barely spared her a glance. ''Nothing to worry about. I work for the United States government. I'm here to ensure your safety.''

For a second, confusion so overwhelmed her she couldn't process his words. Then in an awful moment of comprehension it all began to make sense. She would have preferred a kidnapper. ''Does my father know about this?''

''Senator Barrington is aware we're in a situation where something like this may develop.''

Of course he was. He was bloody aware of everything. He handled everything. Behind her back. Who cared if it concerned her life? At that moment she hated him more than she hated the men shooting at her.

''I don't want your protection.'' She despised the idea of getting sucked back into her father's life again.

''Let me take you someplace safe, bring you up to date. Then, if you still want, you're free to go.''

''I am?'' She stared at him, the wind taken out of her sails. He was logical and had given her the freedom of choice, two things she valued above all others.

"You're not a prisoner." He looked at her, and for the first time she noticed his eyes. They were black or nearly so, bottomless pools devoid of emotion. She looked away first.

"Where are we going?"

He crossed two lanes of traffic, ran off the road, crossed the few yards of grass that served as divider and got on Route 202 going the opposite direction without once putting his foot on the brake. "Lancaster."

She looked back just in time to see the brown van follow and nearly flip over as it hit the divider. Unfortunately, the vehicle slowed for only seconds before resuming the pursuit at full speed. Her fingers fused to the edge of her seat. "To the Amish?"

"Kind of." Swerving across lanes, he executed one evasive maneuver after the other, with the slightest hint of a smile at the corner of his lips.

He probably liked his job. The thought seemed incomprehensible, but must have had at least some truth to it. People usually chose occupations they enjoyed.

Oddly, the smile did not soften his formidable looks. Neither did his worn jeans that stretched over his well-muscled thighs, nor the long-sleeved black T-shirt. He looked very different up-close-and-personal, the deliciously intriguing image of him she had developed during their morning workouts forever ruined by the handgun resting on his thigh.

Her girlish daydreams of him seemed ridiculous now. He was probably a Secret Service agent, everything she didn't want in a man. The bullets bouncing off the hatch window were a good reminder.

The car swerved to the right. He swore in Spanish as he brought it back to the road and steadied the vehicle. "They got the tire."

Her brain held only one thought—it bounced screaming inside her skull. *I am going to die.*

The two men were close behind them, with two guns and a van that would now easily outspeed Alex's SUV. And Alex couldn't even shoot back, it took both hands to keep them on the road with the flat.

"Can you take the wheel?" He threw her an assessing glance.

What other choice did she have? "Yes."

She grabbed on, and they swerved for a moment when he let go and the vehicle jerked to the right. She corrected and brought it back straight and steady.

Alex still had his foot on the gas and kept the speed, much faster than what she would have been comfortable with even if it weren't approaching rush hour, and they didn't have a flat tire and she weren't driving from the passenger seat. Nicola gripped the wheel. She had to handle the car. Their lives depended on it.

Alex rolled down the window and leaned out, his

foot steady on the gas pedal. He fired one shot, then sat back inside and took the wheel from her.

She turned to see the brown van come to a halt in the ditch, its front window shattered.

"How long can we go on a flat?"

"Over thirty miles on these tires." He drove by an exit.

"Shouldn't we get off the highway?"

"Next exit. They'll expect us to take the first."

"You think they'll still come after us?" She felt the blood leave her face at the thought.

"He. The driver is out."

She watched her hands tremble as she rolled down the window a finger width to gulp some fresh air. It didn't help. Nothing would, short of waking up and realizing all this was a dream.

"Are you okay?"

No! She wanted to scream, but was in too much shock to even speak. A couple of seconds went by before she could respond. "You must feel even worse than me. You had to kill a man and it doesn't even have anything to do with you."

Another exit came up, and he took it at the last second without signaling. "You don't have to worry on my account."

His tanned face never flinched. His sharp gaze was fixed on the road before them, but the muscles in his jaw were relaxed, as was the rest of his body. She was having a heart attack and he looked as if he was on his way to breakfast. Of course, the driver of the brown van was probably not his first casualty. The thought did nothing to settle her stomach.

"If they caught up with us, they would have done the same." He spoke to her in an even voice, much like an EMT or policeman trying to calm an upset citizen.

"I know." She closed her eyes, trying to get a grip on what was happening to her life. "It's just that—I'm not used to people getting killed in connection with me."

He nodded as he turned on the global positioning system and rolled onto a narrow country road, raising a billowing cloud of dust behind them.

"How close are we?"

"Not close enough to get there on a flat, if that's what you're asking."

Her hands began to shake again, as her brain downgraded her already-not-too-optimistic forecast for survival. They'd have to walk. And somewhere out there the shooter was still after them.

Alex flipped the car into four-wheel drive then rode off the road into a field of wheat, following what looked like tractor tracks. As the SUV rattled over the uneven ground, she prayed they would reach the cover of the trees before the brown van reappeared on the road behind them. But when they finally got to the trees, finding cover proved to be harder than she had anticipated.

Precious seconds flew by as they searched for an opening in the thick tall brush. Then Alex found it. He pulled the car inside the small patch of woods far enough so they wouldn't be seen from the road, then turned the vehicle so anyone coming after them would be met head-on. When he got out, she followed his example.

"You stay inside." He walked to the back.

"Are you leaving me?" She hadn't considered that. She had thought they would walk to the safe house together. "Are you going for help?"

He looked at her as if she were crazy. "I'm changing the tire."

"Oh." She sagged against a tree.

The heat was oppressive even this early in the day, a physical presence pushing down on her. For days she'd been hoping for a good storm to break the heat wave, some much-needed rain to cool everything off, but according to the weather service there was no relief in sight. She wiped her forehead as she watched the man. If the soaring temperature bothered him, he didn't show it.

He pulled the spare from the back then grabbed the jack. Dappled sunlight glinted off his black hair as he moved with fluid motions. "Get in the car."

Too drained to bristle at being ordered around, she

did as she was told, but left the door open so they could talk and she could breathe. The air stood still in the small grove of trees. "Do you think he'll come after us?"

"Probably."

"Will he find us?" Stupid question. The man, Alex, wasn't a fortune teller. But she was desperate for reassurance.

"Not likely," he said and looked away too quickly.

"But?"

"Nothing."

"If you were him, could you track me down?"

"If someone is determined enough, they'll always find a way."

Great. Bloody peachy.

He snapped the jack into place. "I'm going to make it as hard as I can for him. Don't worry. I think we lost him for now."

He was probably right. It would have taken the shooter a while to move his partner from the wheel, break out the shattered windshield so he could see, and get the van back on the road. Most likely, Alex and she were out of sight by then and the man could only guess where they had gone. Alex had been checking the rearview mirror the whole time. He would have seen the guy if he had managed to catch up with them.

She had to think positively. Couldn't afford to give ground to the panic that fought to take her over, wouldn't allow it to distract her. Not now. She could do this. She had to. She needed to remain calm and ready for whatever was to come.

She felt the car lift from the ground and wanted to offer to get out. She was about to ask but then changed her mind. He had made it clear where he wanted her, and she did feel safer inside. Marginally. She might never feel completely safe again. People were trying to kill her. She wanted back her sane, ordinary world where things like that didn't happen.

He was done in minutes and back in the driver's seat next to her. "Are you ready?"

She wasn't ready for any of this, but they couldn't stay there in the middle of a field. She nodded.

He wiped his dirty hands on his jeans, then turned the key in the ignition, bringing the engine to life. He put his right hand on the wheel. His left held his gun out the open window, the barrel resting on the top of the side-view mirror.

The gesture had such a movie-like feel, she had trouble grasping the reality of it. Just that morning she'd been thinking how well her life was coming along. Sure, she was nobody's idea of a perfect woman and would probably never fit into size-four pants, but she'd learned to live with that. She had a great house, two argumentative zebra finches, and a smoothly running consulting business she'd built with her own two hands.

"I keep thinking I'll wake up to find all this was a nasty dream, brought on by eating too much chocolate before going to bed."

Only when Alex turned to fix his attention on her, his dark eyes intense, did she realize she had spoken out loud. He hesitated for a second, as if weighing her words. He probably thought she was a complete idiot.

But he didn't scoff at her. "That's not going to happen, Nicola. I need you to be able to deal with the here and now." His voice was calm and serious, the expression on his face somber.

She took a steadying breath then nodded as the truth of his words sunk in. She *would* handle whatever came their way. Because her only other option was to die.

Chapter Two

The General's grip tightened on the phone at his ear. "What happened?" How was it possible that the girl had gotten away?

He leaned back in his leather armchair and rubbed the awakening ache behind the barely visible burn marks on his temples where the electrodes had been placed during the endless torture. Since then, when he got tense, he was prone to violent headaches.

"Forgive me, General. There was a man—"

"Get rid of the car and the body." He stumped out his cigar. If someone saved her, it meant she had been watched, protected. He hadn't expected that. A tactical mistake. His enemy was shrewd and the men behind him many. "And don't come in."

"Yes, General."

He got up to pull down some of the bamboo shades, the glaring sunlight aggravating the headache. "Make sure you are caught soon. You know what to say."

"Yes, General." The answer took longer to come this time, but he had no doubt his men would follow his orders—even to their death.

He hung up the phone and looked out into the courtyard patrolled by his soldiers. Today's mission had failed, but the rest of his small team was safe. The authorities would never find them. He knew what he was doing—he was a Meng, descendant of the famous fugitive.

His men would locate the girl again, and this time they would know what they were up against. An armed bodyguard. Maybe more. It didn't matter. They would be ready. He had plans that would change his country, as well as the United States of America. Indeed, they might change the world.

But first he needed Nicola Barrington.

"THIS IS IT?" Nicola stared at the dubious-looking farmhouse as Alex pulled behind the building. The paint on the wood siding had peeled away years ago, only a few brownish-green patches hung on for dear life here and there. At least a third of the roof shingles had permanently departed, window blinds hung broken, and the porch railing appeared to have lain down to rest. The weeds they passed in front were respectable enough for a small jungle. The backyard was no better, dominated by an ancient oak and a dilapidated barn.

The uneasy feeling that had begun somewhere around her midsection when Alex had slowed the car in front of the place grew until tension stiffened her muscles and balled in her stomach. "Do we have to go in?"

"Yes." His foot barely touching the gas, he let the car roll forward on the narrow path of gravel. "It's safer inside. Get down. I'll be right back." He stopped the car and got out, leaving the motor running.

After a split second of hesitation, she did as she'd been told, knowing his orders were for her protection. She didn't have to wait long before he came back and pulled the car into the barn.

He shut off the motor and got out to open the door for her. "We're going in. Stay behind me." He brought two Kevlar vests from the back of the car and handed her one. "Put this on."

She tested the weight—surprisingly light. She had expected it to feel like old-fashioned armor, with steel plates inside, or something similar, but the vest didn't feel like it held metal panels. The material was flexible. She fumbled with the Velcro.

"Hang on." He stepped closer, his voice, despite having kept it low, echoed in the empty barn. "Lift your arm."

She looked away while he secured the bulletproof vest on both sides. The large open space of the barn with all its shadows and smell of moldy hay made her nervous, though she knew he had checked it out before they pulled in. And having him in her personal zone made her jumpy, too. Massive in the shoulders, he towered at least a full foot over her.

She tended to be self-conscious about her height and weight. Richard, her ex-fiancé, had teased her plenty about both. She was "easier to jump over than run around," he used to tell her. She'd stayed with him too long, wanting to please her father. God, she'd been stupid. Nothing she'd ever done pleased the man.

"There." Alex stepped back then put on his own Kevlar before moving outside. He closed the barn door behind them but didn't start out at once. He stayed motionless for several seconds while he surveyed their surroundings. Gun in hand, he led her across the small backyard, always one step ahead of her, shielding her from the road.

When they reached the house, he pushed her to the side, the gun in his right hand, his left on the door. It opened silently and did not, as Nicola had expected, fall off the hinges. The small entryway was dark. She could just make out the second door, solid steel by the looks of it.

Alex pushed a couple of buttons on the numeric

keypad under the doorknob. "This way we don't have to worry about a key."

She followed him into the main part of the house and watched as he disabled the security system. He took off his vest and tossed it in the corner, shaking his head when she wanted to do the same. *Weren't they safe?*

She looked around in the room that showed none of the neglect that plagued the exterior of the building. Tall ceilings, gleaming wood floors, spotless modern furniture and an entertainment system that would have made her own cry in envy. She had expected a card table with folding chairs and maybe a mattress on the floor. But despite the niceness of the place, she couldn't relax. Maybe the house had bad feng shui. She stole a glance at Alex. "Do you come here often?"

"First time."

"Oh." She sat on the edge of the sprawling tan couch and gathered herself. "I'm ready to hear whatever it is you have to say."

"As I told you before, I'm here for your protection."

"I'd like to know your full name."

"Why?"

Good question. To make her feel better? As a reassurance that he and all this was real and she hadn't somehow crossed over into the twilight zone? "Please."

He watched her for a moment. "I can't."

At least he hadn't said, If I told you, I'd have to kill you. "Have you been following me long?"

"Two months or so."

Of course. That was about how long he'd been coming to the gym. "Must have been convenient to get a nice workout and keep an eye on me at the same time." She took a deep breath. "I want to know why."

He leaned against the waist-high counter that separated the living room from a modern and well-equipped kitchen. "We came across intelligence that a U.S. senator and his family might be the target of a terrorist attack. Further investigation picked up your father's name."

Concern leaped in her chest. "Is he okay? Was he attacked?"

He shook his head. "He's being watched 24/7. Any ideas why you'd be a target?"

The word *target* had that cold-knife-in-the-chest feel to it. She rubbed her solar plexus. "Not really. I'd assume it has to do with his position on some hot-button issue. There are always fanatics out there. Did he vote on anything controversial lately? I don't follow his career." She wasn't about to apologize for it or explain further.

"We believe the threat is international."

"China?"

He nodded. "Did he make any enemies while he was there? Anything you remember could be useful."

"He wasn't a popular ambassador." Or rather, the U.S. had been unpopular at the time due to its protective edicts on Taiwan. Her father had been merely the messenger. She swallowed. Wasn't there a saying about shooting the messenger? "He could probably give you more information. I was too young at the time to pay much attention."

"I'm sure he already filled in the case investigators."

She blinked as her brain raced to catch up. Investigators. Right. There'd be those. And God knows what else. Probably press. If there was one thing she hated, it was the media, but under the circumstances that would hardly be avoidable. The events of the morning played in her head in a never-ending loop. "How long do you think I'd have to stay here?"

"Until the shooter is dead or in custody and we figure out whether there are others involved. But even if there are, I don't think another attack is likely. They rarely try to hit the same target twice."

"I vote for that."

He fiddled with the window locks. "In general, terrorists make their point by sowing terror, disrupting people's lives. Sometimes they use the media attention to promote their cause. Whether or not the target dies is almost irrelevant.''

''How nice.'' Good to know there were distinct guidelines to the business.

''Except, of course, for large-scale hits where the magnitude of damage is what they're after and body count is more important. Individual cases like yours tend to be either warnings or revenge related.'' His expression was sober, his eyes assessing every inch of the room while they talked.

''So which one do you think this is?''

He considered for a second. ''Warning. I'm guessing you haven't done much in China that would call for revenge. Your father maybe, but then they'd be going after him. By targeting you, I think they're trying to send him a message.''

''To vote one way or the other on some issue of Chinese interest?''

''Possibly. I'd say they're done with you now.''

She knew he was lying from the way he wouldn't look at her. Probably standard procedure to say something like this to calm down the people being protected—made things easier on him if she didn't become hysterical.

''Great.'' She could stay under house arrest or risk walking into another hail of bullets as soon as she left. Lovely choices. Alex was right about the ''interrupting people's life'' part. She was a business owner. How many clients would she lose if she didn't turn up at scheduled meetings and didn't return phone calls for a week? Her business, assisting reputable Asian companies to break into U.S. markets, was her livelihood. Even if the terrorists didn't come back for her, they could ruin her by simply forcing her into extended hiding.

''Maybe it's not about my father. What if it's related to one of my clients? An unsatisfied customer?'' Although, for the life of her she couldn't think of one.

''I don't think so.''

''How can you be sure?''

''I checked them all out. Thoroughly. And the 'chatter' we came across distinctly indicated the senator.''

He had checked out her clients. Without her consent. She tried not to get upset over that. The man was following orders—probably her father's. And she had to hand it to him, he seemed competent at his job. As much as she hated this whole situation, she was glad she had him on her side. ''Am I allowed to get in contact with anyone while I'm here? Can I use the phone?''

''I'd prefer if you didn't make any calls from this location.'' He moved from window to window like a black shadow as he checked out the front yard.

Staying here in isolation was going to cost her. Big-time. She was supposed to sign the deal of her career on Monday. She had put six months worth of work into convincing CEO Du Shaozu that she was the right consultant to help him bring his innovative game software to the States.

"If you're worried about your business, I might be able to get someone to cancel your appointments as long as you can provide names and phone numbers."

"You could?" His understanding caught her off guard. "Only one that's urgent. I have a meeting first thing Monday morning. It should be canceled today—nobody will be in their offices over the weekend. I don't know the number by heart." But maybe whoever was going to call could look it up. "The name is Du Shaozu at Du Enterprises."

"Right." He nodded, and she had the feeling he knew a lot more about her than he let on. "Anyone else?"

"A half-dozen meetings that I can think of off the top of my head and a few phone conferences."

"Anyone else from China?"

"Several. I'm an international commerce consultant specializing in the Far East. Look, I don't want my clients to be harassed."

"Wouldn't dream of it."

"And there are a couple of friends and my neighbors. They'll definitely notice that I'm missing." She would have to ask someone to feed her finches, although the birds should be fine for today and tomorrow at least.

He shrugged. "Can't risk calling everyone around. They'll just have to worry for a couple of days."

She didn't like it but she understood. "This is serious, isn't it?"

He looked at her for a long moment, probably searching for something reassuring he could tell her. His face was somber as he spoke a single word. "Very."

"I appreciate your honesty." She hated the catch in her voice that made her sound like a frightened schoolgirl. Of course, she *was* frightened. But he probably saw a lot of that in his type of business, had guarded more than his share of frantic women. She would have to try her best not to become one.

"You don't have to worry. You're safe with me," he said.

Her gaze slid over his wide shoulders, the biceps that stretched his black shirt on his arms. He was physically fit, no doubt about that. But even if she didn't have an armed terrorist after her, feeling safe or even remotely comfortable with Alex in the same room would have been impossible.

ALEX SURVEYED THE ROOM for anything he might have missed on the first run. Rectangular, about twenty feet by thirty, it ran the entire length of the house. The living room and kitchen together, nicely fixed up as far as safe houses went. Two windows looked north in the front, one south by the back entry. He opened the first of two closed doors on the east wall and found a hall closet stocked with clothes and other essentials. Excellent. The other door revealed a steep row of rickety stairs to the basement.

He signaled to Nicola to stay where she was, then walked to the landing and turned, only to find the basement walled off. Looked like the job had been done decades ago. He kicked the stones at a couple of places. Solid. No surprises would be coming from there.

He went back up and walked around the room to check out a door under the staircase that led upstairs. A small bathroom with a shower, simple and clean. Packages of toothpaste and toothbrushes along with a few disposable razors occupied the medicine cabinet. A monster of a first-aid kit was tucked under the vanity next to a couple of old Playboy magazines. He grinned. Some things never changed. He closed the door and walked back into the living room.

''Now what?'' Nicola wrinkled her brows as she turned from the window. The Kevlar hid her curves, leaving only her phenomenal legs for him to admire.

They were enough. He could have spent days on those legs alone. Weeks.

The woman was plenty enough to get under his skin and keep him tantalized. He definitely didn't need the magazines under the sink. Best thing for him to do was to drag his mind from that entire direction. He swallowed. "Now I check out the rest of the house."

He ran up the stairs, forcing his thoughts to the work at hand. A steel reinforced door—dead bolt on both sides—closed off the upper floor. Whoever renovated the old farmhouse hadn't bothered with anything beyond that. He scanned one room after the other in quick succession. Not much to look at. The windows were good and locked, but everything else had fallen into disrepair. Drywall full of holes and a leaky roof, no sight of furniture, a gutted bathroom—not a pretty picture. He locked the steel door behind him as he walked back down.

"So?" Nicola was checking out the security system next to the door.

"It's tight."

She nodded, and her silky dark curls slid into her face. She pushed them from her jewel-green eyes. "Are you going to check outside?"

"Not until it gets dark." He clipped his phone off his belt and opened a blank e-mail. "My turn."

"For what?"

"Questions. I want you to give me the name of everyone you came in contact with in China, and as much information about them as you can remember."

"That would take hours."

"Start in order of importance."

She rubbed her temple. "Meng Mei, my best friend. We went to the same school. I lost touch with her after coming back to the States. I don't see what this could possibly have to do with—"

"Keep going." He typed the information into the phone.

"Most of the people I came in contact with worked at the embassy. They went through extensive security clearance, I'm sure. The cooks, the maids, the gardener, the people who staffed the consulate and handled the visa applications." She rattled off a number of names and he took them down.

"Anyone else?"

She named a few of her Chinese classmates at the English language school.

"How about the people your parents came in contact with?"

"Other than the embassy staff, I wouldn't know. I know my father met with a number of Chinese officials, but he didn't talk much about work at home."

"That's fine." The Colonel had probably talked

about that with the senator already. "How about your Chinese acquaintances in this country?"

"About twenty clients currently, but I don't want anyone to contact them." She fixed him with a stern look. "You said you already checked them out."

Her generous lips looked even more tempting when she pursed them like that. "That was before the attack. This is a whole new ball game. They're about to be checked out again." Right down to their great-grandfathers if he had to.

She started to list some names, and he asked as many questions as he could think of, maybe even dragged it out a little. The role felt comfortable, what he was used to. He didn't know what to do after he was done, how to make small talk. It had been years since he'd had to spend more than a night with any one woman, his job not exactly conducive to long-term relationships.

Not that spending a night with Nicola Barrington wasn't more appealing than most anything he could think of. He had spent the past two months memorizing all the spots on her body he would have liked to touch. Seemed harmless at the time, considering they were unlikely to meet. And for damn sure he'd been due some entertainment. Trouble was when night did come, they wouldn't be spending it together in the traditional sense. She would be spending it on the pullout couch while he took brief naps sitting by the window. He didn't expect it to be a particularly satisfying experience.

And the chances of him being able to touch Nicola Barrington under any circumstances were nonexistent. After the next few days, their paths would never cross again. He had no right to be fantasizing about her. Then again, why the hell not? What else did he have?

Nothing. He didn't even exist. Not like other people. He no longer had a social security number, no service record, no contacts beyond his immediate supervisor and occasional teammates. He didn't even have a pair of damned dog tags. Nothing that could identify him. He was part of a shadow created by the U.S. government to deal with problems that could not be handled in open daylight. And when the shadow fell on the people who created those problems, they disappeared.

That was what he was trained for, what he was good at. Not trying to act normal, playing house with a senator's daughter. He sent off the e-mail to Sylvia, Colonel Wilson's secretary, and watched as Nicola rummaged through the refrigerator. Bet she never had to eat food cooked over a camel dung campfire, or breakfast on coconut grubs in the jungle. Had he ever had a normal life? If he had, he couldn't remember it. Certainly not back in Cuba as a young child, and not later, either, once his parents had died and he was left in the care of strangers.

Didn't matter now. All he had to do was keep Nicola Barrington from getting under his skin too much in the next couple of days. Shouldn't take more than that for the rest of his team to pick up the shooter. Between the license plate number for the brown van and the bullets the shooter had left in the pavement at the market, he'd be traced before long.

He should have taken out both men right in the parking lot. Could have from where he was parked, but his primary objective was to keep Nicola safe, which meant getting her away from the attackers rather than engaging them. Damn. He wasn't used to playing the bodyguard. He was more of a seek-and-destroy man.

But guard her he would, even if it meant hiding in the country and sitting on his hands. He would do whatever it took to convince the Colonel that he was ready to be shipped out. He just had to sit tight and refuse to allow her to become a distraction. Piece of cake. He could handle it.

IF SHE HAD TO WATCH Alex do one more push-up, she'd scream. Nicola squirmed on the couch, pretending to read. He did fifty more; with one hand behind his back. Then he started on the sit-ups. She would have had two heart attacks and a stroke by now if she had to do all that. She wasn't very athletic. The only sport she had ever played was baseball, and even at that she was only semi-successful. She was a great pitcher but lousy at running.

She exercised regularly, her Tai Chi and at the gym, but it was nothing like what Alex was doing now. She envied his sinuous body. And lusted after it. In the worst way.

It wouldn't have been so bad if he weren't wearing those stupid butt-hugging Army fatigues he had changed into from his blue jeans and the unnecessarily tight long-sleeved black T-shirt. She, of course, had to make do with an oversize gray drawstring sweatsuit that made her look like a pregnant elephant. Who the hell stocked these safe houses, anyway?

Okay, so maybe it was partially her fault. She had spilled the stupid Ramen noodles on her lap. Not completely without provocation—she'd been severely distracted. He had been taking off his dirt- and grease-covered jeans in the bathroom to put on a pair of complimentary pants from the hall closet. She had found it hard to concentrate on her bowl when the man was getting naked next door.

At least he had let her take off the vest. She had thought she would have to sleep in it. Which brought to mind the sleeping arrangements. She couldn't think of any scenario she felt comfortable with.

Now that she had a chance to calm down, this morning's events didn't seem as scary. The terrorists had made an attempt and missed. The one who still remained would know she was watched and protected. It would be stupid of him to come back.

She wanted her life to return to normal as soon as possible. "Do you think this is really necessary?"

He gave no indication that he heard her.

She hated to be ignored. "If you're my bodyguard that means I am the boss, right?"

He threw her a look that started out as amused, then turned into something else entirely. "If I was your maid or your chauffeur, you'd be the boss."

She thought his voice was unnecessarily sharp. Maybe it was her imagination, but the air seemed to have been charged with electricity between them all day. She had half expected her hair to start standing up. As much as Alex had assured her that he was there to protect her, every time he came near, her instincts screamed, *Run for your life.*

For the past couple of weeks, he'd been an unattainable fantasy, a gorgeous stranger she'd discreetly ogled to take her mind off the pain in her thighs as she suffered on the treadmill. And now here they were. Together.

He was too much—too strong, too tall…too sexy. She had no idea what to do with him, how to relate to him. Men like Alex weren't exactly common in her life. Other than her middle-aged married neighbors, the only men she associated with were strictly business acquaintances. Well, other than Richard, one of her father's aides. But Richard had never made her feel like Alex did. Like she wanted to jump out of her skin.

As the U.S. ambassador's daughter in China, she had been watched constantly, left with few opportunities to socialize with boys her age. When her family had returned to the States, her father had shipped her off to a women's college. Her mother had been gravely ill by then, so she spent her weekends at home missing the coed parties.

Then came Richard the Slime. She must have been pretty pathetic to fall so in love with someone who wanted nothing from her other than her father's favor. After the breakup she'd sworn she wasn't ever going to come within a hundred feet of a government man. It scared her how little judgment she had when it came to the opposite sex—Richard first, and now Alex, some kind of a secret agent.

The key was not to think of him as a man she was attracted to. If she pretended he was a business opponent, maybe she would have better luck with summoning her courage to stand up to him.

She was the one with her life at stake. She wanted to be part of whatever decisions were to be made.

No, not just part of. She wanted to be the one who made them.

"Could we at least go home to get some of my things? I need to keep my business running."

He shook his head.

"It wouldn't take long and you'd be there to protect me."

He ignored her.

"You said I could leave anytime I wanted."

"Didn't want to have to fight with you in the middle of a chase."

She came to her feet. "You lied?"

"You should have known better than to start an argument and try to distract me while people were shooting at us."

"Of all the highhanded—" She moved toward the back door. As indignation filled her, she didn't find him nearly as intimidating. "I can walk out of here right now. I don't need your permission."

He threw her a challenging look. "You think you can get through me?"

Ohh, that did it. "Are you telling me I'm a prisoner and there's nothing I can do about it?" She welcomed the anger that replaced her earlier mix of confused emotions. She felt much more comfortable being angry at the man than mooning after him.

"You're in protective custody. Appreciate it."

She stopped and leaned against the wall with her

arms folded, noting the small dark triangle of sweat on the back of his shirt. Who the hell did he think he was to order her around?

His forehead touched his knees with each sit-up, his combat boots planted firmly on the floor. His movements were smooth and efficient; she could almost feel the tightly coiled power in his body. A military man, no doubt, but tougher and older than the Marines who had guarded the embassy in Beijing. She figured him to be in his mid to late thirties.

"Are you a Navy SEAL?"

He stopped for a moment and looked at her, his dark eyes assessing, the tone of his voice light when he spoke. "Would that make you more comfortable?"

"You telling me the truth would make me feel more comfortable." Although she had less chance of that than a bucket of Häagen-Dazs in hell. That was not how government men operated. Wouldn't recognize a straight answer if it got elected.

"I'm whoever you want me to be," he said, and went back to his workout.

His fingers linked behind his head, he lowered his upper body to the floor then pulled up twisting his torso to touch his right elbow to the left knee, down to the floor, then back again to touch his left elbow to his right knee. He repeated the exercise over and over again without the slightest sign of strain.

He was ignoring her. Frustration tightened her jaw. ‘‘You sound like a cheap prostitute.’’

She was sick of not being told the truth for her own protection. She had worked hard to get away from the suffocating life she had, courtesy of her father. And now somehow she’d gotten sucked back again.

Alex sat on his haunches like a jungle cat ready to pounce. His dark gaze held hers, cold and unyielding. ‘‘Is that what you want?’’

What was he talking about? She had to search her brain to think what she’d said. God, had she just called him a prostitute? ‘‘It’s not what I meant.’’ She watched, rooted to the spot, as he unfolded his enormous frame and moved toward her.

And kept moving closer. ‘‘I—’’ She tried to step away, but it was too late. They were nose to chest, an arm braced on either side of her. She couldn’t do anything but stare at the muscles that bulged under his shirt in front of her face. How did he get there so fast?

‘‘Do you have a problem with me, Nicola?’’ His voice was velvety smooth.

She lifted her chin, and their eyes met. Holy Mother and the Trinity. *He’s a business opponent, he’s a business opponent, he’s a business opponent. This is a professional discussion.*

‘‘No. Of course not.’’ She tried to wiggle away.

Even in business, there were times when the best course of action was to step back a little.

His gaze swept her face. He was measuring her up, testing her. She stiffened her spine and gave him a level look. ‘‘No problem at all.’’

‘‘Good,’’ he replied without letting her go. ‘‘Because we are going to have to work together.’’

Dear Lord, his lips were close. Great lips, but too close. Not at all what you’d expect in a strictly business-type situation.

Chapter Three

She had to focus on something else. Nicola let her gaze slip to his neck, to the tail of what she supposed was a tattoo of a snake disappearing under his shirt. The tail seemed to wiggle with each pulse of the artery underneath and she felt mesmerized by it. She didn't like snakes. Snakes ate birds, and she loved birds. She was definitely losing her mind.

"The finches." She said the first thing she could think of. "They're all alone."

He stepped back.

"We have to get them. What if the terrorists hurt them?" Now that she thought of it, the possibility horrified her. Would they go that far? If they were willing to kill her, they probably wouldn't balk at doing in a couple of defenseless birds. "What if they're kidnapped?"

He pulled up a black eyebrow and watched her closely as if he were trying to determine whether she was serious. ''I don't think that's a worry at this stage.''

''It is for me, damn it! I'm not going to sit here safe and sound while who knows what's happening to them.''

A slight grin played on his lips. ''Politically motivated assassinations of small birds are a relatively rare occurrence.''

''I'm not kidding. At the very least, I need to call my friend to go over and get them.''

He shook his head. ''Not a good idea. I don't want anyone in the house.''

Right. In case the terrorists were hanging around to blow it up. The thought took a moment or two to digest. Her brain wasn't used to running along those lines. She had to keep her girlfriend Sheila out of this.

''I want my babies. My Tweedles need me.'' She hung on to the issue, knowing in the back of her mind that she was probably using the birds to take her thoughts—and his—off more immediate things.

''Tweedles?''

''Umm...Tweedle Dee and Tweedle Dum.'' Shouldn't have said that. Should have stuck with ''birds.'' Okay, so they were stupid names, but when she had first gotten the birds from Richard as a surprise present, she had hated them. With time she had grown to love the bickering pair, but by then the names had stuck.

"Birds are born to survive under rough circumstances. They make it in the wild through periods when there's no food." His voice was full of studied patience, almost to the point of sounding gentle. It was scary.

"Are you crazy? They were born in a cage. Their grandparents' grandparents were born in a cage. They have no fortitude, they have no instincts. Tweedle Dee once tried to hatch a red peanut M&M for over a month."

"Huh?"

"Never mind." She wasn't about to explain the nesting instinct to a man who had so little regard for birds. She had to push him into going somehow. Even if only for a little while, she needed to get out of this house. "I'm going if I have to hitchhike."

He shook his head, not at all looking as if he was buying her false bravado. "Listen to me, lady. You are not going. I am not going. We are not going. Understood?"

"You're scared?"

He swore.

"You don't think you can protect me? That doesn't make me feel all that secure, you know. Maybe you should call for backup." Now that she had miraculously found the strength to stand up to him, she wasn't about to back down.

Color crept up his neck to his face.

"Do you feel incompetent about keeping me safe in general, or only if we have to leave this house for any reason? I'm really not happy about this. I think I need to talk to my father."

Not that she would ask her father for a favor in the next hundred years or so, but Alex didn't have to know that. It seemed important that she regained some semblance of control, that she won at least this one argument.

The vein in his temple bulged as he reached for his cell phone and dialed.

"We're going to need backup." He listened for a few seconds. "Very funny. The lady wants her damn birds. What's the earliest you can get someone to the house? Tell them to give me a call when they get there." Alex closed the phone and clipped it back on his belt. "Anything else you desperately need?"

She gave him a list.

HE COULD TELL it took all her self-control not to gloat. Smart woman. He respected self-control in anyone. He certainly got to exercise his a lot since he'd been around her. His hands itched to glide over those maddening curves that taunted him with her every move.

He turned from her to open the fridge, welcoming the cold air that hit his face. Nothing in there but partially used bottles of ketchup and mustard, and a lonely fuzz-covered pickle in a glass jar on the bottom shelf. He went through the cabinets—Ramen noodles, coffee, tea, sugar, powdered milk, a couple of packages of pasta, paper plates and plastic utensils. Looked dismal so far. Then he hit the jackpot. A double-door cabinet full of MREs. He pulled out a pack with beef stew as the main entrée.

''Would you like one?'' He pointed to the stack of boxes.

''What are they?''

''Meal ready to eat. Military rations. Beef stew, beef ravioli, black bean and rice burrito, meat loaf, chili with macaroni.'' He rattled off a few more options, but she didn't appear particularly impressed.

''Anything organic?''

The worst part was, he knew she wasn't joking.

''It's not gourmet food, but it'll keep you alive.''

The expression on her face spoke volumes.

''If you think this is bad you should have seen the old C-rations.'' He made an attempt at joking.

She showed no sign of appreciation. ''No, thanks.''

''Suit yourself.'' He opened the package then ripped the foil open and made a show of eating his stew as if he enjoyed it, even took the time to reconstitute the dessert with some hot water.

She paged through a stack of old magazines—all on fishing and hunting—on the coffee table, trying not to look at him. He bit back a grin as she failed over and over again. She might have been mad at the sudden turn of events in her life, but she wasn't about to roll over and play dead. She was wrestling for control with him. Cute, in a futile sort of way.

She took a deep breath, put on a stern face and set down the magazine she was holding. "When is the reinforcement coming?"

He took his time chewing and swallowing the stew that had the consistency and flavor of soggy cardboard. "About two hours."

The FBI was probably sending a couple of extra agents along with the bomb squad from Washington. In an emergency, his backup would have come from the Newtown Square FBI Field Office, but the finches hardly warranted the rush. A select group at the FBI headquarters who already knew and worked with the SDDU was preferable to bringing new people into the operation.

Had he needed more substantial help than that, Colonel Wilson might have reassigned other SDDU team members currently on domestic duty, although that would come about only in the direst of circumstances. They were deep undercover in terrorist cells around the country. Pulling them out would have required steep justification.

But of course, he could tell none of this to Nicola, no matter how desperate she was for information. She would never know about his real life, nor the SDDU, of which only two dozen or so—out of the 112 men and six women—served on domestic duty. The rest were scattered around the world trying to stop terrorists before they reached U.S. soil. He couldn't wait to get back.

She cocked her head to the side. "Other than the gym, I haven't seen you around. Where were you?"

He could tell her that much. Didn't see what it could hurt at this point. "Treehouse."

She blinked her gorgeous green eyes. "Zak McKenzie's?"

He nodded. "Too old for playing fort, too young for necking, too smart for sneaking joints."

"He's a good kid."

Better than I was, that's for sure. Alex finished his meal, down to the nutrition-packed power bar, and tossed the packaging. "Neat treehouse. Whenever I can, I take higher ground. The empty place on your other side was tempting, though. It has air-conditioning."

"The Slocskys'? They're on vacation," she said. "Who else was watching?"

"Just me."

"Yeah, right."

He shrugged, not much bothered by what she believed. "Up until today the case was fairly low priority."

If he hadn't been back in the U.S. anyway, to take some time to regain his strength, the FBI would have probably taken the case. It wasn't high risk enough for the SDDU to get involved. More than anything, he was there as a favor from the Colonel, who knew how much he would have hated hanging out at the office and had found a low-key assignment for him.

"No one watched me when you slept? Doesn't seem like thorough work." She pursed her generous lips.

"The security system watched."

"I don't have a security system."

"That you know of." In reality, her house was wrapped in electronics, hooked to his multitasking cell phone that reported any movement on the premises. During the day, she moved around too much for the system to be of any use, but at night the sensors were his eyes and ears, allowing him to rest his own.

"You put up cameras?" Outrage gave surprising strength to her voice.

"Sound and motion sensors."

She seemed to relax at that. She'd probably been worried that he had spied on her in the shower. He felt a fleeting moment of guilt but shook it off. Not his fault, she should have closed the blinds.

"Don't take this as an invasion of privacy. If I hadn't been watching you, I wouldn't have been there in the parking lot this morning."

A quick succession of emotions flashed through her expressive face, and made him wonder if she was remembering the bullets, the driver of the brown van.

"You'll be fine," he said. He should have been able to find something more intelligent to say, but for the life of him he couldn't. He hated the sight of her shoulders sagging as she nodded.

She took a deep breath in a visible effort to pull herself together. "I'm sorry. I shouldn't be treating you like a stalker. You were trying to protect me. I mean, you did. You saved my life. Thank you." She got up and walked over to him, her right hand extended.

He took it, so surprised at her frankness he forgot to let it go.

"I'm sorry I've been such a witch. I just—I have no idea what's going on, and I'm not handling it well, am I?"

"You're doing okay." Another brilliant response. He finally regained his equilibrium and released her hand, immediately missing its soft warmth. "You took it better than most." Not that he knew what other women did in similar situations. Still, she had kept her cool and, aside from demanding the finches, hadn't been much trouble.

Of course, the day was far from over. God only knew what awaited them. That reminded him. "I'm gonna run out to the car. I'll set the alarm behind me. Don't open any doors or windows. Don't turn on the lights."

"Will we have to stay in the dark when night comes?"

He nodded from the door. "We're trying for the abandoned-farmhouse disguise."

He disarmed the system, restarted it, then, gun in hand, opened the door. Nothing moved outside. He stepped out and closed the door behind him before the system armed itself, then walked to the barn, careful to keep in the shadows. The phone on his belt vibrated as he was about to open the barn door. He didn't answer it until he was inside.

"'T's up?"

"The bomb squad cleared the house," the Colonel said on the other end. "The birds will be on their way momentarily. Anything else you need?"

"It would be great if they could grab her some clothes and whatever canned food they can find. Make sure it's organic, although I doubt she has anything else. Oh, yeah, finch food, too, whatever that is. And her electronic organizer and laptop. They're on the desk in her office."

"Comfy mattress? Kitchen sink? Any other amenities you need, Rodriguez?"

Alex killed the line. Nobody harassed him. Not even the Colonel.

NICOLA LOOKED OVER the MREs. Probably sound nutritionally, but she didn't even want to think about the amount of preservatives that must be in each package. Not to mention the calories, designed to fuel the bodies of veritable fighting machines.

She closed the cabinet door as Alex came in carrying a large duffel bag. He set it on the kitchen table and unpacked a pair of gas masks, the sight of which made her stomach lurch. Then came a couple of hand grenades and several rounds of ammunition, night-vision equipment—at least that's what she thought it was—and a jumble of electronic equipment she didn't recognize.

Everything in the pile was there to protect her. Still, the sight of the stuff made her nervous because it suggested they might need those things. She crossed her arms as she watched him pull something else from a side pocket—a small piece of plastic the size and color of a chick pea, and a short unisex hemp necklace with three wooden-looking beads woven into the design.

He held them out in his palm for her. "Let's get you wired."

She cast him a dubious look.

He pointed at the chick pea. ''Ear piece.'' Then at the necklace. ''Microphone.''

''Oh.'' Was he worried that something would happen and they'd get separated?

''I'll help you put them on.''

She wanted to protest, but it was probably a good idea to let him. With her luck, she would have done something backward and then it wouldn't have worked when she needed it. God, she hoped things wouldn't come to that.

She pulled the hair back from her right ear, and he leaned closer to slide the chick pea in. It felt cold at first, but as it took up her body temperature, she barely felt it at all. She turned and held her hair up, away from her neck. Alex's knuckles brushed against her nape as he fastened the necklace. It seemed to take forever. She could feel his warm breath on her exposed skin. A tingling sensation skittered through her body.

And still he wasn't done. He probably wanted to make sure the clasp was secure. His nearness frazzled her. The man had his own force field. She felt zapped every time he came close. ''Is something wrong with it?''

''It's fine.'' He moved away at last. ''Now you're connected to my cell phone.''

''How do I call you?''

''The microphone is voice activated. If we get separated I set my phone to Receiver On. Then when you speak, my phone buzzes to let me know. I should be able to hear everything you say. If I need to reach you, I set the phone on the right channel and talk to you through the ear piece.''

''What's the range on this?''

''It's dependable up to fifty miles, beyond that it tends to cut in and out.'' He looked pleased with himself.

Men and their gadgets. She shook her head, as he moved on to set up the rest of the electronics, attaching sensors to the windows and doors, fiddling with his cell phone as it emitted a series of beeps.

''Isn't the house secure already?''

''For regular stuff.'' Contempt for whatever ''regular stuff'' was rang clear in his voice.

''You're not a regular kind of guy, are you?'' The question slipped.

He gave her an inscrutable look.

She watched as he worked, his movements fast and efficient. He set up both upstairs and down. By the time he did the final walkthrough to survey his handiwork, moonlight peeked through the windows.

He packed up his bag and tossed it in the corner, then grabbed his gun and tucked it into his waistband behind his back. ''I'm going outside for a quick walk around the property. I'll set the system behind me. Why don't you take a shower and relax.''

She hesitated for less than two seconds before she decided to go for it. Having people shoot at you had a way of making anyone sweat, not to mention the muggy heat that showed no sign of letting up. Cool water sure sounded tempting.

She waited until Alex left, then walked into the bathroom. Now what? He had told her not to use any lights, but if she closed the door she couldn't see anything. She could leave the door open to let some moonlight filter in from the living room, but she wasn't prepared to get naked when Alex could come back at any time. She closed the door, put a rolled-up towel at the bottom to block the gap, and turned on the light. Much better.

She took off the necklace, since Alex hadn't said whether it was okay or not to get it wet, but struggled with getting a grip on the earpiece so she decided to leave it in and just be careful. She made quick work of bathing, feeling vulnerable without Alex in the house.

Her only regret was having to put on the same underwear. The only other option, wash it and let it dry until morning, was out of the question. Spending the night with Alex sans undies fell miles outside her comfort zone, even if she had on occasion contemplated just such a possibility while watching him pump iron at the gym.

The man had turned out to be nothing like she'd built him up in her fantasies—a nice-but-fun businessman, gentle, safe. She couldn't handle Rambo.

She turned the light off before she opened the door, then stood there for a second or two until her eyes adjusted to the dark. The living room seemed bigger than before, full of shadows. She moved toward the couch, each step filled with hesitation and nervous readiness to run at the first sign of danger. It was hard not to think about the shooter out there somewhere, coming to finish the job. She sat, not knowing what else to do, her eyes glued to the front windows. What if the man had managed to follow them and had already taken Alex out? What if she was alone? She could be sitting in the crosshairs right now.

And she had forgotten to put the necklace back on. She needed to get it.

A twig cracked outside, and the sound sent her bolting across the room. Her knees trembled as she plastered herself against the north wall. The night seemed quiet again, strangely so. She listened for anything that might have told her someone was outside. A minute went by in complete silence, then another.

Then it felt silly to be standing flat against the wall

like a freeze frame from an action thriller. Sheesh. She couldn't fall apart. Not now. Alex was out there, protecting her. He didn't look the type of man who would be easily taken. The noise outside the window had been probably a squirrel, or the wind, or even Alex, checking the bushes. She had to get it together and gain control of her nerves. She was in a safe house with an armed guard outside. Everything was going to be fine.

She just about convinced herself it was safe to walk to the bathroom for the necklace when she caught a glimpse of a shadow passing by the back window. Her heart lurched and sent blood rushing through her panic-stiffened body. She held her breath as she stared at the spot, but the movement didn't repeat. She waited. Nothing. Was Alex coming back? But then, why didn't he open the door already? What was he waiting for?

Unease lifted the short hairs at her nape and she moved inch by inch into the darkest spot in the room, the shadow of the staircase. She heard some scraping at the door, the noise so faint she wasn't sure if she had just imagined it. Her gaze darted around for a weapon. Where was a baseball bat when you needed one? Or a ball, for that matter. She'd been the best pitcher on the embassy team in China.

A good frying pan would have done as well, but she was too far from the kitchen. No heavy candle holders, either, and not a poker in sight, the living room didn't have a fireplace. The nearest piece of furniture was an end table with a few of the dog-eared magazines she had paged through earlier.

Great. Someone was breaking in and the worst she would be able to do was to give him a paper cut. Moonlight glinted on something half-covered by a magazine—an ashtray. She grabbed it, pleased at the weight of the heavy glass, then watched in wide-eyed alarm as the door opened without sound.

Seconds passed before she could see the dark figure creeping forward—the intruder was shorter than Alex. He looked around, then disarmed the alarm.

So much for security.

The man stole forward in silence, or if he made noise she sure couldn't hear it through the rushing blood in her ears. She had only one chance. She aimed the ashtray for the spot between his eyes and hurled it through the air with all her strength.

ALEX FLIPPED OPEN his vibrating cell phone. Security breach at the back door. Damn it, Nicola. He'd told her to stay put. He moved toward the house, waiting for the alarm to go off. He hadn't shown her how to disarm it for a reason. But as he neared the house, he didn't hear the low-pitched sound, set loud enough only to alert those in the house but not the whole countryside.

Someone had disabled the system. He held his gun at the ready but didn't rush. Couldn't afford to make a mistake now. He set the phone on the right channel to communicate with her. "Nicola?"

No response.

He kept in the shadow of the house, close to the wall. The back door stood open. Nobody outside that he could see. Keeping his body in cover, he looked inside. A dark figure of a man loomed in the living room. He was rising from his knees.

Alex tucked the gun behind his back, not wanting to alert with gunfire the intruder's partners if he had any. He stepped inside, careful not to make any noise, then launched himself at the man. An elbow slammed into his stomach hard, but he'd been ready for it. His right hand went around the man's neck, going for the windpipe.

"*Basta,* Rodriguez, get off me." The muffled words stopped him on the brink of doing permanent damage.

He let go but got his gun ready as he allowed the man to turn around.

"Spike, you dumbass." He stepped back to the door and closed it. "I almost killed you."

"If I wasn't half-knocked-out already, you couldn't have gotten within half a mile of me." Spike limped to the couch.

Alex spotted Nicola pressed against the wall by

the staircase. He stared at her neck. "Where is your necklace?"

"I took it off for the shower."

She was safe. He felt too relieved to be appropriately annoyed. "Don't ever do that again. You all right?"

"Got a bump on my forehead the size of a small egg," Spike answered instead.

"You deserve it. *¿Qué quieres?*"

"The Colonel said to see if you recovered yet."

"He probably meant to ask me, to see if I looked healthy enough. Are you crazy, coming in like that? I could have killed you." He didn't even want to think about it.

"You could have tried." Spike shrugged, cocky as hell.

Alex shook his head and bit back his frustration. Both anger and a lecture would have been wasted on the man. Spike was famous for some of the asinine dares he had taken while they'd been in training together. He'd been a daredevil through and through, had bragged that nothing would cure him of it but a body bag.

"Didn't learn much from cracking your skull, did you? What are you doing in the States?"

The idiot grinned. "Had to deliver a package."

So Spike had brought a terrorist suspect back for interrogation. Alex wondered who it was, what group. Last he knew, Spike was trying to take down an Arab cell in Germany. Sounded like he had a successful mission.

Alex envied the man. This glorified baby-sitting—hiding from the terrorists rather than going after them—went against every instinct he had, not to mention his training. "Did you check out the market in Devon?"

"They used an Uzi, not what I call a hot lead. Anyone can buy those on the Internet since the Soviet Union broke up. Not much of a shooter. The bullets went way high."

"Do you work with Alex?" Nicola spoke finally.

"God forbid."

"Sorry about the ashtray."

"Don't mention it." Spike grinned. "Good aim."

"Did you get my birds?"

"Yeah. They're fine. I pulled the car off the road about a mile east of here. Wanted to see how good the protection was you were getting. With Alex being in a 'delicate' condition and all, the Colonel was wondering if you might need a real man on the job."

"I'll show you real." Alex moved toward him.

Spike maneuvered around the couch and out of his grasp, his blue eyes sparkling with humor. "I better go bring in your stuff."

Alex had half a mind to go after him just to see if he'd learned any new moves since they'd last seen each other, but then thought better of it. No sense acting like two immature schoolboys in front of Nicola. "Pull into the barn, there's plenty of room."

He watched the man walk out the door and rub his swollen forehead. At least he could find some satisfaction in that. Nicola had brought Spike down. The lady definitely bore watching.

After Spike had gone, he gave credit where credit was due. "Well done," he said, unable to resist a grin. He liked a woman who could take care of herself. Of course, to be truthful, he liked most everything about Nicola.

She grinned back, her face bathed in moonlight, her silhouette accented against the window. It reminded him of a specific fantasy he'd spent considerable time on during the unbearably slow nights in the treehouse. In his mind he had explored every tempting inch of her body— He caught himself and shelved that particular memory. Those were things he needed to forget instead of dwelling on them. He was here to do a job. That's what he had to focus on.

Not an easy task. She was dangerous in the moonlight—and not just to his libido. He grinned again. It would be a long time before he would let Spike live down the ashtray. Nailed by a civilian—a woman at that. "Have to remember not to turn my back to you."

She smiled innocently, wide-eyed, but he wasn't buying any of it. Not even when she said, "I wouldn't hurt you. We're on the same team."

Sounded strange coming out of her mouth. He wasn't much of a team player, worked mostly lone-wolf infiltration. Takedowns that required teamwork were few and far between. But in the three years since the SDDU came into being, they had taken more than a hundred terrorists out of the picture and stopped dozens of attacks. Unfortunately, as soon as they neutralized one bad guy, two took his place. SDDU soldiers fought against insurmountable odds in operations that the American public and the rest of the world knew nothing about.

And he preferred it that way. He wasn't in it for the glory. The job had to be done and he had the skills to do it. He had no family depending on him; he could afford to risk more than others. The work was its own reward—the rush of adrenaline, the test of his mind and body against others, the satisfaction of knowing that he made a difference. He didn't need anything beyond that, didn't miss a thankful public, and certainly didn't want any medals. The anonymity suited him well.

He hoped that in a week, two at most, he'd be back out there working on a new mission. It would have to be a good one to make him forget Nicola Barrington.

Chapter Four

Nicola set the towel-covered cage on the counter and took a peek at the Tweedles. They were a little ruffled but otherwise fine. She felt better having them with her, even though the bomb squad cleared her house and Spike had assured her it didn't look like the terrorist had been there.

"When can I go home?"

Spike lifted a large bag onto the table, similar to Alex's. He was well built, not as tall as Alex, but still had a formidable look to him. Short sandy hair, a strong jaw, steel-blue eyes—he was probably handsome under normal circumstances. Hard to tell, with the large bump on the middle of his forehead and the redness spreading from it.

"When we can be sure there'll be no more attacks coming. In the meanwhile, you'll be leaving for Washington sometime tomorrow. We have better facilities down there."

Translation: "Can't give you specifics for your own good, and by the way, this safe house is not all that safe so we have to take you to another one."

She looked at Alex. He didn't seem to be jumping for joy, either. Couldn't blame him really. For the first time, she considered things from his point of view. He was stuck in a godforsaken farmhouse with a complete stranger. Probably not his idea of fun. And yet, he would protect her, risk his life for her if needed. She had never understood that kind of dedication.

What made certain people hand their entire lives over to the government? What motivated her father to pack up his wife and daughter and drag them all the way to China? To sign away their freedom? Living within the embassy walls and guarded by Marines, being watched twenty-four hours a day was as bad as being in a prison.

Her mother hadn't liked it, either. Couldn't handle the pressures coming from both the U.S. and Chinese governments. She had tired of the endless functions that stole her time from her daughter and any other interests she might have had in life. Nicola had been perceptive enough even at that age to notice the stress. Sometimes she wondered if under different circumstances her mother would have been able to put up a better fight against the cancer.

''Is my father in a safe house? Does he know what happened here?''

Spike pulled out a bag of finch food and handed it to her. ''He knows, but he's keeping his schedule. We added extra staff to his normal security detail.''

''I see.'' She resisted asking if he had a message for her, if Senator Barrington had expressed any concern over the assassination attempt on his daughter's life. If he had, she was sure Spike would have passed it on.

He pulled some clothes from the bag and it took her a second to realize they were hers. Underwear, too, the really skimpy ones from the ''just in case'' pile she never got to wear. Some still had tags on. ''Thanks.'' She blushed and grabbed them off the table when she caught Alex openly staring.

Next came a dozen or so cans—ravioli, chili, soups—all organic. Excellent. She hadn't remembered to ask for those, but was grateful that Spike had thought of it.

He pulled out her laptop, the last item in the bag. Then he reached into his shirt pocket. She could have cried in joy when he handed over her electronic organizer. She hadn't remembered to ask for that, either. She'd been on the frazzled side when she'd made up her wish list.

She had half a dozen appointments this week, in addition to the one with Du Shaozu on Monday. She had worked long and hard on those accounts. "Thank you. You might have saved my business."

Spike shrugged. "Thank Alex. He called in the shopping list."

Of course. After having watched her every move for two months there was probably little the man didn't know about her. The thought made her uncomfortable. Her privacy had been violated, and for that she had trouble feeling thankful.

Alex lifted his hand in the no-thanks-necessary gesture, solving that problem for her.

"I don't suppose I could use your phone?" She turned back to Spike to push her luck.

"I'd rather you didn't, but if you put together a list of people and give it to me I could probably arrange for someone to call them for you."

Same response as Alex had given. She would have to make do. "It'll only take me a minute." She rummaged through the kitchen drawers until she found a pen, then copied the most essential names and numbers to a napkin from her electronic address book.

"Had to leave town on urgent business, will be in touch at the earliest opportunity," Alex dictated to Spike as he glanced at his watch then flipped on the TV.

The eleven-o'clock news came on and they didn't have to wait long before the anchor got to the shooting in Devon. He called it a drive-by, without mentioning her, the rescuing vehicle or the fate of the attackers.

"You had a bouquet of flowers by your door," Spike said. "From a gentleman by the name of Du Shaozu."

"A new client. Flowers? Can I see them?"

"No," Alex said.

"They're out in the car in an evidence bag." Spike threw him a curious look.

Alex flipped the TV off and came around to check out the birds. "Kind of scraggly, aren't they?"

In her usual abrupt manner, Tweedle Dee backed up to the bars and squirted, barely missing him. Nicola winced. So much for making a good first impression.

Alex took a quick step back. "Hey, I think I've just been insulted."

"You know, a lot of people have that kind of opinion of you, Rodriguez," Spike needled him.

"Oh, yeah?" Alex pulled up to full height, but then smirked at Spike. "What kind of opinion will they have of you when they find out a girl did you in with an ashtray?"

Spike cleared his throat. "Um…I'd appreciate it if you didn't mention—"

His ringing cell phone cut him off. He listened to the caller for a few seconds, then handed the phone to Nicola. "Your father. They've got him on a secure line."

Among the slew of emotions that swirled inside her, relief was the strongest, surprise a close second.

"Are you okay?" they said at the same time.

"I'm fine," she said as her father waited. "Somebody tried to shoot me this morning." Her knees went weak as the words brought back the memory.

"I know. Are you okay?" he asked again.

"They missed." She walked to the living room so she could sit on the sofa. "I'm a little shaken, but I think I'm safe now."

"You are. I've been assured that you have the best protection. Just sit still. Is there anything you need?"

She couldn't remember the last time she heard him this worried over her. Over bills, vetoes, votes, sure. But not her.

"I'm sorry I'm not there for you. They wouldn't let me come."

"It's fine. Really. I'm taken care of," she said after a moment, resorting in her surprise to her old if-you-don't-want-me-that's-fine-because-I'm-self-sufficient-and-I-don't-need-you routine.

Except that right now it seemed he really did care and wanted to know that she was all right. She didn't doubt the sincerity of his concern, but it didn't make up for the years of neglect. And it was hard to forget that she was in this situation because of his job, a job she'd hated since she'd been a child.

"Tomorrow I'm going to—"

"Listen, I better go now," she said, cutting him off. She was glad to hear he was well, but beyond that they had little to say to each other. "Take care of yourself. Be careful."

She could hear him take a deep breath.

"You, too," he said.

NOT HAPPY TO SEE his SUV go, Alex watched Spike drive down the long driveway without turning on the lights. Now he was stuck with Spike's black sports car—faster than the SUV, but not nearly as good on dirt roads if things came to that again. Unfortunately, since the shooter already knew his vehicle, he had no choice but to trade it for the Batmobile that screamed its owner had more testosterone than common sense.

No, that wasn't true. Spike had plenty of common sense, just not when it came to danger or cars or women. Still, Alex trusted few men as he trusted him. When it came down to the wire, the man knew how to get things done.

He had asked him to check out Shaozu, even though he itched to do it himself. After some pressing, Nicola had admitted to a couple of business lunches with the man. More than was warranted, in

Alex's opinion. And now the flowers. He didn't like the idea of Shaozu sniffing around her.

He turned back into the house, locked the door and set the security system. Didn't look forward to the night. Spending it in the same room with Nicola gave him zero chance of sleep. He looked up at the sound of her feet on the stairs as she came down.

"There's nothing up there."

He tried not to laugh at her accusing tone. She had probably gone up to check out the sleeping arrangements. Had to be awkward for her, too, first time with a live-in bodyguard. He wished he knew what to say to set her at ease, but he wasn't exactly at ease himself.

"Where will we sleep?"

Leave it to her to tackle the question head-on. He liked that about her, the unflinching honesty and guts to face things even if they were uncomfortable. "You take the pullout sofa, I'll make do." He carried a chair to the window and settled into it. He was used to sleeping in a sitting position.

Nicola looked over the sofa, then began to set it up. He didn't offer to help. She managed fine on her own. The farther he kept from her, the better. "Sheets and pillows are in the hall closet."

Once they were in Washington, the Colonel would round up some extra bodyguards from the FBI to share shifts. He might even be able to talk the man into letting him go after the shooter. Not that he didn't think Spike capable. Spike was good, maybe even better than him for this particular operation. He spoke both Mandarin and Cantonese, in addition to another dozen or so languages. He had come to the SDDU from the FBI's language program.

Alex had come from the Army Special Forces. He and the others, Rangers, Marines, SEALs, Special Agents, had their old connections, making it easy for the SDDU to draw on the strength of a variety of organizations. That was the beauty of the SDDU—its people. The Department of Homeland Security had handpicked them from the best sources.

Nicola was lucky, even though she would never know who protected her. Alex leaned back in the chair, folded his hands behind his head and stretched his legs.

She finished the bed and was settling in for sleep. Without a blanket. The night was definitely warm. He turned his head toward the window to find a safer view.

NICOLA WOKE to the sound of running water. Couldn't have been more than four or four-thirty, judging from the faint light of dawn outside. She was used to getting up early, especially on the days when she worked out, but today it pained her. It seemed they'd only gone to sleep a few minutes ago.

She looked toward the source of the noise. The bathroom door was open—probably so Alex could keep an eye on things while he showered. And he was definitely showering. She could see him through the clear glass.

Oh, my.

Standing with his back to her, he bent to shut off the tap. She had trouble breathing. He straightened and shook the water out of his hair, then pushed the door open.

The dim light of dawn showed enough to be overwhelmed by the outlines of well-muscled limbs, the curve of his buttocks as he turned, the width of his shoulders. He reached for the towel and looked right at her.

She felt powerless to do anything but stare, her mouth so dry it hurt to swallow.

He toweled the water off his body with unhurried movements, got dressed in the clothes he'd left on the back of the toilet, then went over to the sink for a shave. She looked away finally, then with full muscle control regained, threw herself into activity. She had the bed made up by the time he finished.

"I...you...could have closed the door," she managed to say when he walked out into the living room, then felt stupid as soon as the words left her mouth.

His gaze bore into hers and held. "You could have turned around."

Nicola flushed. Touché.

She yanked the towel off the finch cage, grasping for those last fleeting shreds of her dignity, and welcomed the instant bickering that filled the silence.

"Those two hate each other or what?"

"Pretty much. They fight over the nest."

"They have two."

"I know. They both want the same one."

"Captivity can bring out the weird in anyone."

Tell me about it. She tapped the cage as Tweedle Dum pulled a puff of feathers from Tweedle Dee. They quieted at the noise, but she knew the peace would be temporary.

Alex picked a can from the counter and began to open it. Even under the long-sleeved black shirt, she could make out the play of muscles on his back.

She needed to think about something else. "Chili for breakfast?"

The birds kicked off a new argument.

"Probably better than any of the MREs." He seemed focused on the can opener.

Good. They were on a whole new track now, the shower incident forgotten. By him anyhow. It would take her more than one lifetime. "When are we leaving for Washington?"

"As soon as we get the call." He dumped the chili into a pot and turned on the stove. "You should get some more sleep."

"I'm fine. I can sleep in the car."

He nodded as he stirred. "You can't go outside for your Tai Chi. You'll have to make do in here."

Oh, Lord, had he watched her every morning? She'd practiced religiously since Mei, her best friend in China, had taught her years ago. "I think I'll skip." Tai Chi was about relaxation as much as movement. Relaxing. Ha!

She'd seen him naked.

She doubted she would be able to relax by the time she was old enough to be a grandmother.

Get a grip. She couldn't think about Alex's naked body. She had to focus on staying alive. She had to find out as much as she could about her situation.

"Is Spike on your team?"

"Yeah. Kind of."

"I suppose I would have expected more activity after a terrorist attack." She hadn't even had to file a police report. That seemed odd. Wasn't there some kind of protocol to follow when someone almost got shot into mosquito netting?

"There's more going on than you know. Right now the FBI is doing everything to find the guy."

"Are you FBI?" She fiddled with her necklace.

"Something like that."

Another meaningless answer, when she'd thought she was finally getting somewhere.

"You're not going to tell me, are you?" She tried

to temper her frustration, but being kept in the dark was almost as bad as being in danger.

If she didn't know what was going on, she couldn't very well make good decisions, decisions on which her life depended. She thoroughly resented the fact that her father and some unknown organization presumed to know what was best for her.

"So you've noticed me at the gym," he said out of the blue, making her forget that she was about to call him onto the carpet on the secrecy issue.

Must be he didn't think she'd had enough embarrassment for one day yet. "You grunt when you bench press."

"I do not."

"Do, too. Starting at about two hundred pounds."

He quirked a black eyebrow, his gaze steady on her face as he stirred the pot on the stove. "You watched me that closely, huh?"

She chose to ignore him. The aroma of spices filled the kitchen, but her stomach, clenched into a tight fist as it was, couldn't properly appreciate it.

He pulled the food off the stove and brought it over.

"No, thanks." She put her hand on the disposable plastic bowl he had set out for her. "I'll try one of those MREs. Figure it's my once-in-a-lifetime chance."

''If you're lucky.'' He grinned and piled the chili into his bowl.

She got up to find something among the rations that sounded remotely tolerable. They ate breakfast at quarter after four, spicy organic chili and beef ravioli in the semidarkness.

Her toes tingled under the table.

WHEN THEY STILL hadn't gotten the call by noon, Nicola was worried. Alex had spent the day obsessively checking the property and the sensors, while she tried just as obsessively to keep out of his way.

''Do you think something went wrong?'' she asked when she couldn't take the silence any longer. Maybe the terrorists had attacked her father and the FBI had forgotten all about her. Her chest tightened at the thought.

''I'm in no hurry,'' Alex said, flat on his back, his hands behind his head. He sat up, his nose touching his knees. ''The closer I am to Washington, the more likely someone will snag me—'' he lay back down ''—to write one of those loathsome reports.'' He came up again.

He stopped his sit-ups and reached for his phone, and she thought he was going to call after all, but he started to speak into it as soon as he flipped it open. They must have buzzed him.

''Ready?'' He listened to whoever was speaking

on the other end. "Can't they send someone else?" He listened again then swore before he ended the call.

"Time to leave for D.C.?"

He shook his head. "They got the shooter. He's singing like a bird. He and his brother were on some personal vendetta against your father. You're going home."

She needed a moment to adjust to going back to her normal life so abruptly. From one moment to the next everything kept changing. She didn't have the kind of skills it took to handle such chaos. She'd barely accepted for real that she'd been attacked, and now apparently she was out of danger. God, she was getting whiplash.

Oh, what the hell was wrong with her, feeling disgruntled because things were changing too fast? The authorities got the shooter. She could go home. She waited for the rush of relief, but it didn't come.

Shooter in custody or not, it would take time to regain her sense of security.

"I'll be going home all by myself?" The thought of being alone after what had happened yesterday was less than comforting. "I guess now that everything is back to normal... I don't suppose—"

Since she had raised such a fuss about him guarding her in the first place, it would probably have looked pretty stupid if she begged him to stay with her a little longer.

"I'm coming with you to spend the rest of the week," he said with a barely disguised groan before he left the house to collect his sensors.

Oh, thank God. "We're going home, babies," she whispered to the finches bickering on the coffee table, oblivious to the sudden end of danger. If there were any ruffled feathers among the three of them, they were definitely hers.

ALEX PARKED on the other side of the street for a while. Nothing suspicious. He scrolled through the fields on his cell phone. Spike had set the security after he'd left Nicola's house. Didn't look like there had been a breach.

He pushed a button, and the garage door opened.

"How did you do that?" Nicola stared at his phone.

He grinned at her astonishment and slipped into his pocket the special-edition cell phone that had saved his life on more than one occasion. He pulled into the driveway, then into the garage next to Nicola's car.

"How did my car get back?"

"Spike." He closed the garage door.

"May I take the vest off?"

"No."

"Why?"

"Your windows aren't bulletproof." He got out with his gun drawn. "You stay behind me."

"I hate being a prisoner in my own home. Hated it as a child, did whatever I could to get away from it as an adult. Doesn't look like it worked, does it? All I wanted was some freedom."

"I understand." And he did. For him it was second nature to be always looking over his shoulder. But Nicola was a civilian; she wasn't used to this. Nor should she have to be.

"What about the Tweedles?" She hesitated to follow him.

"Let's check the house first." It didn't seem smart to bring noisy birds along while they tried to sneak around. He didn't expect any surprises in there, but he wasn't about to take any chances.

"Okay."

"You have to admit it's strange that someone who values freedom as much as you do would keep caged birds as pets. Kind of symbolic, don't you think?"

She gave him a funny look. "For your information, they were a gift. And they like their cage."

He crooked his eyebrow.

"That's what they're familiar with. They wouldn't know what to do outside. Probably couldn't even find food. I am not being mean to them."

"I didn't say you were." He lifted his finger to

his lips to signal to her to be quiet as he opened the door that connected the garage with the house.

He wasn't satisfied until he checked everything from basement to attic. Then he set out to double the sensors, and let her get on with whatever it was she wanted to do, while he kept an eye on her. Despite frustration over his baby-sitting assignment being extended, watching Nicola Barrington move around the house was by far the most enjoyable task he'd had lately. After Yemen, maybe fate figured it owed him a good turn. He wasn't going to question it.

She was incredibly feminine. Not in the sense of femininely fragile, but head-to-toe real woman. He couldn't be near her and not be aware of her, aware that he was a man. She was a contradiction—all soft curves on the outside, but on the inside the kind of quiet strength rare even among men. At every turn she had stepped up to the plate. She'd had the presence of mind to get into his car and away from the terrorists, held the wheel while he stopped them from following, defended herself against Spike. Her life had been taken apart then put back together again in the last twenty-four hours and her eyes never teared.

Alex watched as she brought the finches in from the attached garage—he had allowed her free movement as long as she didn't go outside. As soon as she set the cage on its stand and pulled the cover up, the birds began to chirp and fly around, which pretty soon escalated into another fight over the nest. She appeased them with some seeds, then walked out to the kitchen, her movements as graceful as a dancer's. Another thing he liked about her—the fluidity of her stride, the easy flow of limbs with which she accomplished even the most ordinary tasks. Probably came from her Tai Chi practice. He wondered if she'd gotten into the habit of her daily morning exercise while she lived in China.

She moved on to the kitchen and, to his regret, out of sight. Pots rattled. Dinner? He'd forgotten that neither of them had eaten since lunch, eight hours ago. Now that the noises filtering in from the kitchen reminded him, his stomach growled for attention. After countless months of existing on MREs, he would have given anything for a home-cooked meal.

He fought the urge to go in there to watch her. Instead, he went outside to check on the sensors he'd set around the perimeter of her property and added a few extras, wishing the Colonel would call with an update. He would have liked to know more about what the captured gunman had said.

THE GENERAL SET DOWN his teacup and turned his head to escape the pungent odor of its contents. The mixture of Chinese herbs was great for his headaches, but the taste was hard to tolerate. But then, one often had to put up with a certain amount of unpleasantness to get results. "Are you sure?"

"Yes, General."

Was it a trap? He had hoped his plan would work, but hadn't expected Nicola back so fast. She'd been hidden somewhere near. They committed their first mistake—underestimated their enemy. Good position for him to be in. "Must not miss this time. Move as soon as you are ready."

"Yes, General."

He pushed the cup away. He wouldn't need the rest of his herbal tea tonight. Good news was the best medicine.

Soon victory would be his, and China would be free. He regretted that things had to come this far, but it wasn't his fault. The U.S. government was to blame. He had asked for help nicely, he and thousands of other Chinese. But the U.S. refused to help the Chinese people to break free from the tyranny of their communist government.

There was too much money invested in China by American businessmen. The last thing they wanted was political upheaval and uncertainty. And powerful businessmen had powerful lobbies. They paid for elections. They owned senators. And for that, help was withheld from his people.

He was done begging.

If the U.S. had taught the world one thing in the

past few years, it was that countries that harbored terrorists and were the source of terrorist activity, would be dealt with swiftly, their governments deposed, their people liberated.

He knew what he had to do. Orchestrate a terrorist attack of such magnitude that the U.S. government would have no choice but to respond to China, the source.

Nicola Barrington was just the beginning.

Chapter Five

With the sun finally down, the air felt marginally cooler in the backyard, although still far from comfortable. But despite the luxury of a running air conditioner in Nicola's house, Alex didn't want to go back inside. Or rather, he wanted to go back too much and was smart enough to know it wasn't a good idea. He needed something to distract him from Nicola.

It was just like Spike to have taken her skimpiest clothes to the safe house to tease him. She was still wearing the shorts and a tank top from that batch, completely covered by the too-large Kevlar vest. With not an inch of clothes showing, she looked as if she was naked underneath. Might as well have been naked altogether. His overactive and overstarved imagination provided him with tantalizing details.

Maybe she'd change. Probably not, though. It had

to be pushing a hundred degrees outside; he couldn't see her putting on long sleeves and pants anytime soon.

He took a deep breath, then another. They didn't help. The air was as hot as the woman inside.

The yard secured, he checked out the street and the neighboring properties as he fiddled with his phone. A quick call. He punched the number.

Colonel Wilson picked up on the second ring. "Everything all right?"

"Just wondering if you had any developments."

"Nothing that would help us. The man the FBI picked up is Xu Jinsong. Citizen of the People's Republic of China. He entered the U.S. two weeks ago on a tourist visa. We've contacted the Chinese Embassy and requested his criminal record if any. Still waiting."

"Is the FBI still questioning him?"

"I put Spike on the job. Everything the man said has checked out so far, though. Looks like this case is over."

Good news at last. Besides being a language whiz, Spike was also one tough SOB. If Xu was hiding something, Alex had no doubt Spike could make his bird sing before long.

"Everything all right?" the Colonel asked again. "Anxious to get back to Yemen?"

"Yeah," he said, surprised to find that had not been the real reason for his call.

"Might be sooner than we thought. We have a new situation developing. One of the microbiologists we've been tracking in Saudi went for a visit to your old Yemeni friends, then disappeared."

"Who's on the job?"

"Baker. He followed the man from Saudi, but I need him back there."

"When will I be going?"

"I'm still waiting on a couple of things, but it shouldn't be long. Looks like the Barrington case is about ready to be rolled up. I'll let you know when I have a date."

"Thank you, Colonel." He closed the phone and clipped it back on his belt. Good news all around. In a few days Nicola's life would be back to normal and he'd be back in the action. Oddly, it didn't fill him with as much excitement as he'd thought it would.

Nicola filled him with excitement—the unprofessional kind. Now that it seemed the danger was over, he had a hard time maintaining the kind of focused vigilance it took to keep his mind off her. Since he didn't have to look over his shoulder every second, he found himself looking at her more and more often. And he was experienced enough to know that wandering eyes tended to lead to wandering hands, and that led to…someplace he was definitely not going to go.

NICOLA SET THE TABLE, turning at the sound of Alex coming in. He looked pensive. Probably ready to move on to the next adventure. He stopped to inhale the aroma of Szechuan chicken cooking in the wok, but didn't say anything.

The sight of him sniffing around her stove was so domestic, her brain had trouble processing it. Just two days ago, she'd been dodging bullets with him. It had been only two months since she'd first seen him at the gym. And now he was living in her house. A temporary but nevertheless mind-boggling arrangement.

"Dinner will be ready in another fifteen minutes." She laid a pair of chopsticks next to her flat square plate and another pair next to Alex's. Then, on second thought, she added a fork to his place setting.

He leaned his long frame against the countertop and watched her; she could feel his gaze on her back even after she'd turned to get some glasses.

"Wine?" She pulled a bottle from the rack and held it up for him. She didn't drink often, but enjoyed a glass of nice dry red now and again, and every once in a while a satisfied client presented her with something special.

The Bordeaux in her hand had been a gift from

Du Shaozu, a charming, intelligent man with plenty of vision. She looked forward to working with Du Enterprises soon. Now that the shooter was in custody, she might even be able to keep her original appointment with Shaozu in the morning. Of course, as busy as the man was, the empty spot on his calendar had probably been filled in immediately. Nicola set the bottle on the countertop. She had the hardest time thinking about work while Alex watched her.

"No rice beer?" He eyed the wine, his lips tugged into a slight teasing grin.

He didn't smile much, but when he did, it sure looked good on him.

"Fresh out." She handed him a corkscrew from the top drawer.

"What will you do if it goes to my head?"

Oh, dear. Was he serious? The last thing she wanted was for him to lose control.

Or was it?

He pulled the cork and poured, then handed her a glass, his fingers touching hers.

She pulled back, then lifted the glass and took a nervous gulp, too rattled to enjoy the sweet wine on her tongue. He seemed to have no trouble savoring his. She watched as he set his glass aside after a few careful sips.

The contents of the wok sizzled behind her.

Sheesh, she'd forgotten to stir. Thankfully, it didn't burn. She took care of the meal and gulped some more wine, trying not to look at Alex.

"Nervous?"

Jittery was more like it. She made some noncommittal sounds.

"You don't have to be. I'm here."

Precisely.

"Refill?" He picked up the bottle and brought it over.

Had she finished her glass already? Lord, he probably thought she was a guzzler. Oh, what the hell. She held her glass out. She needed to relax. Any more tense and her fingers would snap the bamboo spoon she was using to stir the food.

His gaze flickered over her while he filled her glass, his eyes two swirling black pools. Something in them that… Couldn't be. She must have been imagining it. She offered him a nervous smile. Men like Alex never checked her out, not even under normal circumstances, and right now her best features were both covered under the Kevlar vest. She looked like SpongeBob Square Top.

He didn't step back after he poured. "You are the most desirable woman I've ever met," he spoke the words slowly, deliberately.

She took a sip. A large one.

"Nicola?" His voice was smooth as Chinese silk gliding over her skin.

She took another sip. Boy did she need it. She kept the wineglass between them as a shield.

He put his hand on hers and drew the glass to the side as he stepped closer. She had no place to go. If she moved back any further she'd be sitting on the stove. And she was plenty hot already. Only because of the dratted vest. Yeah, right.

His gaze never left her face as he lowered his mouth to hers.

The kiss lasted only a second, leaving her lips tingling as if she'd bitten into a hot pepper. But instead of wanting to run for a drink of cold water, she wanted more; she wanted all of it.

He set her glass on the counter. "I shouldn't do this," he said, then gathered her against his mile-wide chest and kissed her into oblivion.

His warm lips teased with skill, and had her at the point of mindless abandon within seconds. Her mouth parted with pleasure as he advanced, a military man clearly well versed in the art of invasion. He tasted of wine and passion, a heady combination that went straight to her head. She had to hang on to his shoulders for support.

He must have foreseen the problem of her weakening knees, the good soldier that he was, because he picked her up and set her on an empty spot on the counter. His tongue did things to hers that probably fell under "strictly classified" for the protection of the masses. Civilization itself would have been in jeopardy if all men kissed like this. Women would never have let them leave the house.

His lips teased, promising everything then delivering more, sending delicious shivers through her body. He trailed kisses down her neck as far as the vest allowed, then up to take her earlobe a prisoner of war. Giving no thought to the Geneva Convention, he engaged in exquisite torture.

"Hot," he mumbled against her sensitive skin, "...in here."

Yeah. She knew what he meant. The air conditioner was going full blast, but she didn't feel any of it. They generated plenty of heat between them. His muscles shifted under her fingertips as he moved. She ran her hands down his arms covered in one of his standard black long-sleeved shirts.

"You could take this off." Had she said that? Had she just asked the most gorgeous man she knew, top secret agent, special military commando, to take his shirt off in her kitchen?

His gaze, thick with passion, held hers while he considered, but then he moved forward and kissed her again instead. She didn't have time to be disappointed. The kiss was full of hot need and frustration, melting whatever measly defenses she might have had left. He possessed her, and she gladly gave herself to him. Would have given it all in that moment of madness had he asked.

She leaned into him as his hands ran up the outside of her thighs, waking up every nerve ending along the way. She used to wish she could suck them in as one sucked in one's stomach, wanting just once to look down and see knobby knees. But judging from the sounds coming from deep down Alex's throat, he thought her legs were just fine. And then, next thing she knew, they were wrapped around his waist.

He pulled his gun from his waistband and set it on the counter, then returned his full attention to her. His long fingers maneuvered in purposeful caresses on her skin until she was ready to jump out of it, or at least out of the inconvenient bulletproof vest that stood between them. She teetered on the brink of pure bliss and frustration, wanting more, more, more.

Once again, he anticipated her. He sneaked a hand under the vest until he found what he was looking for, and she moaned into his mouth, her body ready for surrender. His palm pressed against her breast as he ran his thumb lightly over her nipple.

He devoured her lips. She could feel the proof of his desire hard against her. Yes, she thought. This is what she wanted. This is what every atom of her body was screaming for. The pleasure of his hands on her body took her breath away.

Then the realization hit her. The Kevlar might protect her against bullets, but she had no protection whatsoever against her bodyguard.

THE SMELL OF BURNING soy sauce brought them around.

Alex drew back from her, his growling stomach forgotten long ago. The hot hunger inside him ached for Nicola alone. He licked his lips to capture one last taste of her and waited for her to say something, something other that what a mistake this has been. As far as he was concerned, he would be damned if he'd apologize.

Nothing but the sizzle of the wok broke the silence between them.

She wouldn't look at him as she slid off the counter. "I better get that."

His gaze ran up her legs and he already missed the feel of them around his waist. He looked at her arms and wished they were still wrapped around his neck. He couldn't see much more than that from the blasted vest, too stingy to show the curvy delights his hands had found. Her silky dark curls bounced around her face as she bustled between the stove and the table. For a second he caught a glimpse of her seductive lips that had been his downfall. They were still swollen from his kiss.

The sight of them was almost more than he could bear.

He took their wineglasses to the table to give his hands an occupation other than grabbing her, and willed his raging blood under control. The Colonel hadn't sounded the all-clear yet, and until then, Alex couldn't afford to be distracted from the job he was here to do. And *distracted* was hardly sufficient to describe the thousand pains of desire that swarmed inside him like angry bees in a hive, leaving his aroused body buzzing.

His gaze followed her as she placed the wok on the table, then sat across from him, and for a moment he could almost imagine his life like this. A woman, somebody permanent who moved gracefully in his life, cooked mouthwatering meals, kissed him dizzy before dinner, then loved him senseless after.

Not a bad fantasy.

Too bad it could never happen. He was a lone wolf. Officially. Said so in his psychological assessment, one of the reasons why he'd been offered a spot in the SDDU. The character traits and skills he had were suited for guerrilla warfare, not for playing house in suburbia. He probably wouldn't have liked that kind of life, anyhow. No sense getting all sentimental about it.

All he had with Nicola were a few more days at

most. He would enjoy them while they lasted, but he could never forget that he lived in a different reality.

He heaped chicken and vegetables on his plate, but the phone buzzing on his belt stopped him from picking up his fork. He got the phone out and flipped it open. ''Perimeter breach. Front. Get down.''

He grabbed his gun from the counter, turned off the lights, then went to the window. A group of boys played street hockey outside in the twilight. Zak McKenzie ran out of the bushes that divided his parents' property from Nicola's, threw the puck to one of the players and the game resumed.

''Just a couple of kids.'' He turned on the light.

Nicola got up from behind the counter and scowled at him. ''I hate this.''

''I know. It'll be over soon.''

She took up her chopsticks, and he grabbed his fork ready for the food.

''It's great,'' he said after the first spicy burst of flavors diffused in his mouth. ''You could get men to do anything for cooking like this.''

''Actually, I can do most everything myself pretty well, thank you.

''Great. Just my luck. An independent woman.'' He grinned.

''What's wrong with that?''

''Nothing. Independent women are my favorite. But every once in a while it's good to feel needed.''

"You protect me," she said.

"That I do." *But I'd like to do so much more.*

The phone buzzed on the table where he'd put it.

"Yeah, yeah, get down. I know the drill." Nicola crouched next to her seat.

"Front." He shut off the light and went to the window in time to see another kid chase after the runaway puck on Nicola's lawn.

"We're fine." He turned on the light.

She sat back at the table. "You're upsetting my digestion," she said, but her voice didn't have any bite to it.

The phone buzzed six more times before it got dark enough so the kids went home. He checked each time, not taking any chances.

They were doing the dishes when he realized the acrid smell in the kitchen was getting stronger and it wasn't coming from the pot with the burnt soy sauce on the bottom. "Stay here."

He ran through the rooms downstairs, stopping at the door that connected the laundry room to the garage, and saw the faint lines of smoke coming through the gaps. He put his hand to the wood. It singed his palm.

The phone buzzed as he ran back to the kitchen. "The garage is on fire."

"What?" Nicola started for the back door, but he pulled her back and flipped the phone open.

Perimeter breach, back, side, front. One after the other. ''Can't go outside. They've got us surrounded.''

He pulled her from the kitchen, and she grabbed the cage, as he pushed her up the stairs in front of him, dialing the Colonel. ''We're under attack,'' he said as soon as the other side picked up, then ended the call and turned to Nicola.

''I want you to barricade yourself in your room.''

''What about you?''

''I'm going to make sure no one comes up.'' The narrow staircase was a good spot to defend. He could see anyone coming into the living room, and nobody could get behind him. He could take them out before the fire spread to the main part of the house.

''Then take the vest.'' She tugged at the snaps.

''No.'' He pushed her back.

Something small rolled toward the foot of the stairs and caught his eyes. ''Tear gas grenade. Go!''

He could have probably still protected the stairs for a while, his training had included the tear gas chamber, but he wouldn't have been able to function at full capacity and he wasn't about to take any chances with Nicola's life. Had he been in combat gear, he would have had a gas mask on his belt, but as it was he had no option other than to abandon the stairs and follow Nicola into the bedroom.

''Stay down.'' He locked the door behind them,

rolled up a small area rug and pushed it against the crack, then blocked it with her dresser.

No doubt the Colonel had sent the FBI and the local police, but it would be a while before they got there. He wanted nothing more than to walk through that door with gun blazing and take out those SOBs. But he couldn't start a shootout, he couldn't risk Nicola. Hot frustration tore at him when another emotion, one he'd never experienced with such intensity before, slammed into his chest and brought him to a halt—fear.

Fear for Nicola's life.

He couldn't afford to think about that now. Alex shrugged off all emotion and turned his brain to "commando mode." He searched the backyard through her balcony door, but saw no movement. "Stay behind me." He opened the French doors slowly.

He scanned the shadows of the night, his ears trained on the noises downstairs, people moving through the house. In a minute or two they would clear the lower level and come upstairs to find her.

Still nothing moved in the yard, but he couldn't risk going down and being seen through the windows. Nor could he risk walking into whatever trap might be waiting for them in the bushes.

He placed his hands on her shoulders, his stomach

knotting at the sight of her wide-eyed fear. "I'm not going to let anything happen to you."

She nodded.

"How are you at climbing?"

"Never really tried." She looked down. "It's not that high. I could probably jump."

He got on the railing. "We're going up."

"What about the birds?"

"We have to leave them. The fire department will be here long before the flames get this far. I can't risk them making some noise and giving away our position."

To her credit, she set the cage in the far corner of the balcony without arguing, and opened the door. They waited a few seconds, but the birds showed no sign of wanting to take advantage of their sudden freedom.

"We have to go." He reached for the gutter and tested it, then swung himself up. He lay on his stomach and held his hand out for her. She followed without hesitation, her knees trembling as she stood on the balcony railing, holding on to the downspout for support. She couldn't reach the roof, but she could reach his hand. He pulled her up as she braced her feet on the siding and "walked" to him.

Once her head was level with the low-pitched roof, he came up into a squatting position and hoisted her up. She lay on her stomach panting, but he couldn't give her much time to rest. He could hear someone slam against her bedroom door, trying to break it down.

"We have to go over the top." He reached for her hand.

He moved fast, crouching as low as he could, pulling her behind. Too fast probably, but he didn't have a choice. Her bedroom door shattered. Even over the popping fire in the garage, he heard the dresser crash.

They made it over the peak and flattened themselves against the rough asphalt shingles. The next second he heard someone yell on the balcony in a language he couldn't understand.

With his hands, he signaled to Nicola to start sliding further down, until they were far enough so they could come up in a crouch again without being seen from the other side.

He watched as a chunk of the garage roof caved in, the supporting beams destroyed by the flames below. The rest seemed to be holding up better. The narrow strip by the edge in front of them remained untouched, leading to a majestic oak on the other side of the house. The giant branches stretched from the garage to the neighbor's solid wood privacy fence.

"Figures. The garage is the only place in the house where I didn't have a smoke alarm," Nicola said, calmer than he would have expected.

They had to move on. He could see people, two

of them, fanning out to search her front yard below. If he had thought they were the only ones on the property, he would have taken them out on the spot. But he heard voices from the house, and there must have been others, as well, in the backyard. Not too many though—somewhere between half a dozen to a dozen men altogether. Odds he would have gladly taken on were he alone.

He moved across the garage roof, bending low, gun in one hand, Nicola's clammy fingers in the other. The fire rose high next to them, its searing heat making their flight even more difficult. He glanced at Nicola and swore at the sight of her trembling figure as she stared at the flames. "Almost there." He tugged her along. "Keep your eyes on my feet. Step where I step." He wasn't sure if she could hear him over the fire now that they were directly next to it.

What the hell was he thinking, bringing a civilian up to a burning roof? If the terrorists didn't kill her, his carelessness probably would. She wasn't trained to do this. He didn't know the first thing about protective custody. He protected civilians by going to the bad guys and taking them out before they got into the country. He prayed his mistakes wouldn't cost Nicola her life.

They got to the tree just as another chunk of the roof collapsed. He lifted Nicola until she had a secure hold on a branch thick enough to support their combined weight and was able to climb onto it. He reached up to follow her when he felt the roof shake again.

The beam he'd been standing on gave way to crash into the flames below. And took him with it.

Chapter Six

No! Nicola stared after Alex as he disappeared into the fire and smoke. She lay on the branch, holding it in a death grip, too stunned to scream. ‘‘Alex?’’ she whispered toward her necklace a couple of times and waited in vain to hear his voice in her ear.

Heat and smoke rose through the gaping hole in the roof in waves. Nobody could survive the inferno below. Tears filled her eyes, but even through them she could see men on the ground, dark shadows moving through the night. They were going in and out of the house, checking behind every tree and bush of the yard—a pack of predators hunting. Only a matter of time before one of them would look up and see her illuminated by the flames.

And even if that wasn't a concern, the flames certainly were. They crept closer and licked higher with every passing second. She loosened her grip on the branch and inched backward. She didn't have to worry about not making any noise. The fire below had been rapidly growing, and now drowned out every other sound.

The closer she got to the trunk, the wider the branch became, making movement easier. Then she reached the fork and sat inside it for a few seconds to gather her breath, the picture of Alex falling back into the flames stuck in her mind, filling her with horror. She couldn't go on. Not without him. What was the point? She'd never make it.

Try, her mother's voice said in her head. Try what? Slipping onto the ground was out of the question—way too much activity down below for that. She would have to make it over the neighbor's fence to the other side. She was pretty sure that had been Alex's intention. She couldn't do it.

Alex had thought she could.

She sucked in a breath, grabbed onto the widest branch going in the right direction and began to climb. She reached the fence fairly fast, pushed to rush by the smoke blowing in her direction. She coughed and hoped it wouldn't be heard below, although she doubted anyone could see her through the smoke, even if they did look up.

She finally reached the fence and lowered herself onto a thick post, then slid down to the neighbor's yard and crouched behind a sprawling azalea bush. Her hands shook, as did her legs and her insides, her throat raw from smoke. She wiped the tears from her eyes so she could see, and looked toward the street, wanting more than anything to get up, run around the fence and go back to the garage to help Alex.

If she thought he had one chance in a million to be still alive, she would have. But she didn't. She couldn't delude herself. She'd seen that fire. Still, she called his name into the microphone again.

Nothing.

She crumbled against the fence. On the other side, Alex, a complete stranger until a few days ago, had died for her. He could have climbed onto the tree first to pull her up after him. He hadn't. He'd put her life first, died so that she would live.

And he'd done it without thinking, without hesitation. That's the kind of man he was—gruff at times but constant and reliable, putting her safety before his own. Losing him hurt. Nicola hugged her knees as pain washed over her. Alex was gone—his rare grins, his arrogant confidence, his way of making her feel safe. She grappled with the thought as she stared into the night with tear-soaked eyes. Physical attraction aside, in all this madness, she had come to care for him.

The Slocskys' empty house stood a few yards in front of her. Her neighbors, a lovely retired couple, spent their summers at their beach house at the Jersey Shore. Alex would have probably taken advantage of that. Maybe she could get inside, out from the open where she would be spotted as soon as the attackers decided to widen their search.

She pulled herself together and stood, brushed the tears from her eyes so she could see as clearly as the night allowed. She darted behind a hemlock tree next to the house, then stopped to scan the deep shadows of the patio. Nothing there but the familiar topiaries. She turned around to check the front but caught a movement from the corner of her eye and froze.

A dark figure, black from head to toe including the mask that covered his face, moved toward her. He stopped and looked around, took another couple of steps then stopped again. He hadn't seen her. He would have come straight to her if he had. She tried to control her nerves enough to think. She still had a chance.

She willed him to turn around, to choose another direction. But instead of following her telepathic suggestions, he inched closer still.

Another couple of yards and it'd be over. The fire next door gave off enough light for him to see her. She held her breath. Maybe if she stepped back closer to the wall, deeper into the shadows. The slight movement might attract the man's attention, but as it was, another few steps and he would see her anyhow. What did she have to lose?

She crept back without turning, connecting with

the wall sooner than she had expected. It moved. At the same time, a hand clamped over her mouth from behind.

ALEX PUT HIS OTHER ARM around hers to hold her still. If she struggled or made any noise at all, they would be discovered. He placed his lips on her neck below her ears in a brief kiss, trusting she would understand his message, know it was him. They had been kissing, minutes before the attack. He hoped she would make the connection. He couldn't risk whispering in her ear, and even if he managed to noiselessly turn her around, he doubted she would recognize him as he was, covered in soot from head to toe.

After a moment, he felt her sag against him and he let her go. He needed his hands for other things. Most importantly, to get the gun he'd taken away from one of the attackers.

He had run into one of the terrorists as he dragged himself out the back door of the garage, his clothes smoldering. That guy wouldn't be bothering anyone again. But as much as he had wished, he couldn't go after the rest. His first objective was Nicola. He had to be by her side to guard her. He couldn't kill all the attackers at once, and one could get to Nicola before he got to all of them.

She stiffened in his arms, and he watched as the

man took another step forward. Then another. Alex raised his gun. One more step and he would have to take the guy out, and then the sound of gunfire was sure to bring the rest running. If it came to that, they would have to be fast.

He got ready to shove Nicola behind him and shoot at the same time. His finger rested on the trigger.

Sirens filled the air.

The man looked around, then ran back in the direction he'd come from. Alex relaxed his arm as the sirens grew louder. The fire company came first, then the police a few seconds later. He stayed in place, holding Nicola with one arm to him.

"It's me," he finally whispered into her ear.

"I know." She turned in his arms and hugged him tight, hanging on for dear life.

He had a Russian-made Makarov—a fine gun at that—in one hand, and a woman he had no business holding in the other. And they were not out of the woods yet. The terrorists were probably still out there, watching, while he had no car to get away.

"Mrs. Slocsky's Oldsmobile is in the garage." Nicola lifted her head.

He nodded and held her back from going straight for the door, not wanting to set off the light hooked to a motion detector. He went in through a window instead, helped her in, then turned off the outside light and unscrewed the bulb in the garage that was probably set to turn on when the garage door opened.

Hot-wiring the car took seconds. He clicked the garage door opener clipped on the back of the sun visor, then, without turning the headlights on, backed out onto the driveway. An empty police car blocked their exit. Not a problem. A few bumps and a couple of flowerbeds later, he rolled off the next-door neighbor's driveway to the street and drove in the opposite direction from all the commotion, ignoring the small groups of neighbors gathered in their robes and pajamas. A couple of them were talking to the police, looking dazed or worried.

A police car took off after him almost immediately.

"Damn."

Nicola looked back. "What? Police is good, right?"

"Not now. We can't afford to stick around to explain things. We'd be sitting ducks for a sniper." He glanced at the flashing lights in his rearview mirror as he floored the gas pedal and pulled ahead. He had to get away before the cops had a chance to call for backup.

After ten minutes of hide-and-seek and racing down side streets, he killed the headlights and pulled into an empty carport. The cruiser came around the corner the next second and zoomed by behind them.

As soon as it disappeared from sight, Alex took off the other way. "I think we're okay."

Nicola leaned back in her seat. "I'm so glad you're here. Back at the house when you fell—I thought—" Her voice sounded off, high-pitched.

Alex kept an eye on the rearview mirror. He'd never had anyone worry about what happened to him on a mission before. He didn't like the idea of Nicola being anxious over him, and he liked even less the possibility of him thinking about her and making a mistake, maybe not taking a chance he should have.

And he'd been worried about her, too, blamed himself for letting her out of his sight. He had fallen with the roof, leaving her alone for nearly ten minutes, giving the terrorists a thousand chances to kill her. He didn't like the cold pain that spread through his stomach at the thought.

He unclipped the cell phone from his belt and handed it to Nicola.

"See if you can get this to work. I think I fell on it. Couldn't reach you earlier."

She fiddled with the thing for a while and pushed buttons. "Nope. Keypad is cracked and the front cover is partially melted. I think your phone is broken."

She closed the cover and set the phone on the seat between them. He reached for it to clip it back on his belt. If it didn't contain more confidential information than a secret agent could uncover in a year's hard work, he would have chucked it out the window.

He had lost his car, his gun, his phone. He was pretty much cleared out. It wouldn't stop him, but it would slow him down. And that was the last thing he needed right now.

Nicola opened the glove compartment and handed him an old cell phone. "Here. Mrs. Slocsky keeps it for road emergencies. I think this qualifies as one. She probably wouldn't mind."

He looked at her for a long moment before he took the phone. First she'd gotten him the car, now this. She was beginning to feel almost like a partner.

He turned on the phone and glanced at the screen that warned him about the low battery. *Figures.* Still, all he needed were a few seconds. He dialed, relieved to hear the ring on the other side. "We're on our way back to the safe house. One enemy down," he said as soon as the Colonel picked up, not sure how long the battery would last.

"Are you both all right?" The man's voice came in a hiss of static.

"Affirmative."

"Spike's still here. I'll send him over to check the place out and pick up that body. I'll let you know if he finds anything."

"I'd appreciate that."

No sooner had he put down the phone, than he noticed the tail. They were out on the main highway now, not as many cars on the road this late. The Jeep was catching up with them fast despite his best efforts to outrun it, the Oldsmobile's six cylinders no match for the other's eight.

Could be an undercover cop car. Maybe the officer he'd lost back in Devon called in his license plate. Then the Jeep pulled closer behind them and he saw the semiautomatic in the passenger-side window. Definitely not standard police issue. He pushed the gas pedal as far as it went, but the advantage he gained was temporary. They were on him within minutes, this time with bullets flying. He swerved, but it didn't seem to help. The back window took a hit and shattered. He felt something prick his shoulder.

"Are you okay?" He glanced at Nicola. She was bent over her knees, head down, but gave him a thumbs-up.

It pissed him off that she was getting to be such a pro at being shot at. She shouldn't have to be. She should be able to ride in a car without having to keep her head down. She had the right to a normal life.

And he would see to it that she got hers back before this was all over.

The guy behind them squeezed off another round. Damn. Alex swerved. Where was his bulletproof SUV when he needed it? And where was his SIG, more accurate than the Makarov he had commandeered at the house? He doubted he could pick off the driver as cleanly as he had the other day.

He grabbed the gun and glanced at Nicola, half expecting her to protest at having another man killed on her account. Civilians were funny that way sometimes. Took them a while to catch up with the game.

"I'll hold the wheel." She took over with a look of fierce determination, before he had the chance to ask.

He gave her a grateful look, then rolled down the window and stuck his head out. The man behind them sent forth another round. Nicola kept the car steady. Alex squeezed off a couple of shots at the bastard, then more at the Jeep's windshield and radiator. There. That slowed them right down.

Once again he waited a couple of exits before he got off the highway, making sure they weren't being followed, then took side roads to backtrack to the safe house.

He took the same precautions as the day before, parking in the barn, checking the house once they were in, then walking the property after seeing to it that Nicola was safely settled in. Everything seemed in order.

He pulled her into the bathroom with him after he came inside, closed the door, tucked a rolled-up towel in the gap by the floor, then turned on the light.

"Just want to check if you're okay." He looked over her face, legs and arms but found nothing other than smudges of dirt and soot, a few minor scrapes from the shingles that had been as rough as sandpaper. "You look—" The alarm on her face cut off the rest of his words. "What?"

"You're burned all over."

NICOLA STARED at the red welts on the back of his hands and on his neck. "Oh my God." On his right arm, the material of his shirt had melted onto the burned skin.

He pulled at it and winced. "You know, it didn't hurt that bad until you pointed it out." He let the shirt go. "Damn."

"You need to go to a hospital." And right away. All she knew about burns was that they were extremely painful.

He looked at her as if she were crazy. "That's not an option."

"Then I'm going to take care of it." She meant that as a threat.

He nodded. "Do you know anything about treating burns?"

"Nothing. You should go to a hospital. Your wounds are probably getting infected as we speak."

Her medical knowledge consisted of a handful of Chinese herbs Mei had helped her plant in the embassy garden. They had gone to the same English language high school with other children of foreign diplomats and high-ranking Chinese officials. And even those herbs, were she able to get them here, wouldn't have helped. They had been selected by Mei to help Ambassador Barrington's constant indigestion. Nicola knew squat about burns.

"Emergency room?" she suggested again, hoping he'd see reason.

"I trust you to take good care of me." He bent to open the cabinet under the sink and pulled out the giant first-aid kit. "We've got all this."

She opened the box and stared at the contents, a jumble of drugs and bandages that overwhelmed her. And that was before she saw the surgical instruments, IV bags and syringes.

"That one is good for pulling bullets." He pointed to a sterile bag that held a pair of long scissors with tweezer-like tips.

Yikes. She picked out a pair of scissors, the ordinary kind. First things first.

"What do you think you are doing with that?" He stared at her.

"I'm cutting off your clothes."

A muscle twitched in his soot-covered face. "My shirt."

"Yes."

She started with a nice clean cut right up the middle, then realized the shirt was soaking wet on his right arm. She hadn't immediately seen that on the black cloth. "Why are you wet?"

He brushed his hand against the shoulder and the sleeve came away torn, his palm smeared with blood.

"Oh my God." She peeled away more of the material that had been held in place by dried blood. There was plenty of fresh blood, too, trickling down his arm.

Alex took a closer look then shrugged. "Stray bullet."

"You could have told me you were shot." The man carried the macho thing too far.

"Grazed." He grabbed a towel and dabbed at the wound.

A week ago, looking at something like that would have made her pass out. Now all she felt was concern for Alex. Amazing how two terrorist attacks in two days could harden a person right up.

"I really think you need medical attention." Surely he couldn't be so stubborn as to not realize that.

"And that's what you're gonna give me." Alex pointed at the first-aid kit. He grabbed the shirt where she had stopped cutting, ripped it the rest of the way, then pulled it off his left arm and held it so it wouldn't tug the skin on the right.

She hooked the scissor under the sleeve and cut

away as much as she could around the melted area. Once she was finished, she grabbed the tweezers from the kit and looked at Alex. He held her gaze without blinking, his face set in a hard mask.

She lifted the edge of the burned piece of cloth expecting the worst, but for once it seemed they caught a break. "It's just melted into your hair, not your skin." She tugged with the tweezers.

"Why don't you try one of the surgical knives?"

She cut the coarse hair, mindful of the reddened skin underneath. Even with a knife as sharp as she used, it had to hurt, but Alex didn't make a sound.

When she was done, she looked over the rest of him quickly to see if he had any other injuries, but the grime of blood and soot made it hard to assess the damage. His broad chest appeared to be fine. His burns seemed to be in places where his shirt hadn't protected his skin. No other bullet wounds that she could see. Not that the one on his shoulder wasn't enough.

"Does anything else hurt?" She glanced at his pants.

"I'll check the rest myself." He looked down, and soot fell from his hair, some of it landing on the open wound on his shoulder.

"We need to get you clean."

"I'll hop in the shower."

"I don't think water hitting those burns is going to feel good."

"Let me worry about that." He turned off the light and pushed her out the door.

She stayed just outside so she would hear if he lost consciousness from the pain and hit the floor. A good fifteen minutes passed by before she heard the water turn off.

"Would you mind getting me something clean to wear?" he called out, making her jump.

She walked over to the hall closet, rummaged through it, and settled on a large pair of sweatpants. They had even stocked packages of underwear. She opened a multicolored six-pack and pulled out black briefs. She didn't grab any of the T-shirts. She needed to treat his wounds before he put anything on top.

She knocked, and he opened the door a few inches. The light was off inside, and she absolutely, positively couldn't see a thing, but her hands still trembled as she handed him the clothes.

"Thanks."

He didn't bother with the door.

"You can come in," he said a minute later.

She made sure the door was closed behind her before she turned on the light.

"No injuries below the belt," he said.

Thank God for that. Then she wouldn't have to

treat anything in that area. She washed her hands in the sink with soap, twice, then looked over the burns on his neck and hands. He also had a cut on his forehead the dirt had hidden. His worst injury seemed to be the gash on his right shoulder that was still bleeding liberally. Nothing looked life threatening, but what did she know?

Alex rummaged through the kit. "We just need some disinfectant."

"I'll do it." She took the bottle from him and swabbed the wound, then let him walk her through stopping the bleeding and bandaging his shoulder.

"How about the burns?" she asked when she was done.

"Should be a bottle of Pentametlin in there."

She looked through the drugs and came across one by that name in a medium-size white canister, much like a can of hairspray.

"What is it?"

"A white foam that contains a combination of five different kinds of disinfectants, burn medications and local anesthetics."

"Do I just spray it on?"

"Liberally."

She started with the left hand. "What do I use for a bandage?"

"Nothing. It's better to let it breathe as long as

I'm just lounging around the house and there's not much chance of dirt getting into it.''

She nodded as she moved on to the other hand then the neck, working next to the tail of his tattoo snake as it curved around from his back.

''Turn around.''

''No.''

The sudden harshness in his voice surprised her. ''I want to see if there's any other damage.''

''There isn't.''

''Damn it, Alex. I'm not going to stab you in the back.'' Did he have some hideous birthmark? Or was he embarrassed by the rest of his tattoo? Did he think she would care?

He looked into her eyes, his expression set in stone. Then he turned.

His tattoo stopped on his shoulder as if the tail was part of a painting of a snake, the rest of which had been erased. His entire back was a giant scar, not new and red like the others in front, but healed over white wells of agony and torture. A startled gasp escaped her throat. Her reaction made him flinch.

She reached out a finger to touch him, unable to believe her eyes. ''Alex…''

He spun around, his dark gaze boring into hers. ''Satisfied?''

He reached over her and shut off the light, then pushed by her and walked out into the living room, leaving her alone in the dark. What had they done to him? Rage and sympathy filled her at the same time. Who could do such a thing to another human being?

"You can't go yet." Her voice was weak, her mind stunned at the thought of the terrible pain he must have suffered. When he had said he was recuperating from an injury, she had figured he meant a broken rib or two, or a bullet wound at the worst. What on earth could make anyone go back into a job that had left him like that? "Wait. I have to treat the cut on your head."

His only response was a grunt.

Good enough. She'd take that as an agreement. If he was too stubborn to go to the hospital, he would be forced to put up with her. Nicola washed the foam off her hands, dried them, then rummaged through the first-aid kit in the dim moonlight that filtered into the bathroom. She picked out a tube of disinfectant cream and a couple of butterfly bandages.

She found him by the window and watched him for a moment as he stared outside, his imposing figure illuminated by the light of the full moon. He had put on a T-shirt from the hall closet.

She took a deep breath. "Alex?"

He sat as still as if he'd been carved from rock. He did not respond.

"Everything okay?"

He nodded then.

"I need to look at your forehead. It'll only take a minute." She moved closer, half expecting him to tell her where to go, but he turned sideways to allow her to proceed and bent his head to give her easier access.

She pushed his wet hair out of the way and spread some cream on the wound, grateful for the moonlight that made her work possible. His skin had been sliced by something sharp, probably as he'd fallen with the garage roof. But on closer inspection, the cut wasn't as bad as she'd first thought. Three butterfly bandages were enough to hold it together.

"That's better." She screwed the top back on the tube and smiled at him.

"Thank you." He did not smile back, the expression on his face unreadable.

Then she saw his neck, the spot where the T-shirt rubbed against the burn and had already taken off most of the medicine. That wouldn't do. "Hang on for a second."

She returned to the bathroom, dropped the cream and extra bandages back in the kit, and grabbed the scissors and the Pentametlin. She wanted to do whatever she could to help him. Although he did not complain, he had to be in pain. Easing it to the best of her abilities was the least she could do. Especially after all he'd done for her.

He waited by the window. On duty. He never

stopped, did he? She thanked God for that. It was the only reason she was still alive. She knew precious little about the man, but she knew this: as long as he breathed, he would guard her with his life.

"Let me cut around the neck of that T-shirt so it doesn't rub against anything sensitive."

"Have a thing for cutting clothes off me, huh?" The hard look disappeared from his face suddenly, and he flashed her a cocky grin.

She was smart enough not to go there. Instead of giving him an answer and fanning his ego, she made quick work of the shirt and reapplied the medicine. He leaned forward, his head inches away, his dark gaze searching her face before it settled on her lips.

They tingled in anticipation. It was insane. He hadn't even touched her yet. "Um, I should—" She had no idea what she should do, only knew what she wanted to do, wanted more than to take her next breath.

He ran his hands up her bare arms in a gentle caress, and her mind went blank. In that moment nothing existed but the two of them in the moonlight. She lost herself in his touch, in the swirling black pools of his gaze that drew her to him irresistibly.

"Nicola," he whispered her name into the night, the sound soft and light, running across her skin like dancing butterflies.

And she knew he was going to kiss her.

Chapter Seven

Alex drank in the picture before him—Nicola's upturned face in the moonlight, her wide-eyed expression as she read his intent, her full lips parting on their own. If there was a man on this earth who could resist such temptation, it sure as hell wasn't him.

Mad for a taste of her, he took what she willingly offered, not because he was aroused—hell, he'd been that from the day he'd first seen her—but because he needed her. He needed to feel her to know they were both truly alive.

Her mouth was soft and warm, making him forget every one of the dozens of reasons why he shouldn't be doing this. Then she brought her hands around his waist and kissed him back, and he couldn't remember anything ever feeling this right.

His fingers ached to roam her body, but the Kevlar blocked them at every turn. She still wore the vest, and without her clothes showing, she still looked naked under it. The thought still drove him crazy.

She moved to take off the vest but he held her hands still. She definitely needed that for protection. From him.

While she wore that vest, she was safe. Reasonably. He couldn't guarantee that she'd be completely safe from him as long as they were on the same continent.

He kissed her eyes, then covered the rest of her beautiful face in kisses before moving on to her neck and ears, aching to go on, wanting more, so much more. Her lips searched his and he obliged them gladly, drinking in her sweet taste. Having spent plenty of time in the desert, he knew what true thirst was, but he had never been as thirsty for water as he was for her.

She sneaked her hands under his T-shirt, over his abdomen, up his rib cage, and her light caresses left him mindless with desire. And then it got worse. She brushed her fingers over his chest, his nipples, and he sucked in his breath, afraid if she did much more he might explode.

But when her hands wandered to his back, he froze.

"Alex?"

In his mind he could see her delicate hands touching the loathsome welts that had once been his skin, and waited for her to recoil. Then he couldn't wait any longer and pulled away.

"I'm sorry." She moved toward him.

He moved back.

"How did it happen?"

"Leave it, Nicola." He hesitated for a second, then stood and set her aside. "I'm going to check outside."

He walked away without looking at her. Distance was what he needed and a little fresh air to clear his head. But his head had a hell of a time clearing. He shivered in the balmy night as he walked the perimeter to check for anything suspicious. He took his time. Only when he couldn't find any more excuses to linger, did he go back in.

She had already opened the couch and was lying under a thin sheet. She didn't move as he walked by her to take up his post by the window. Good. She was sleeping or pretending, he didn't much care which as long as she stayed away. He didn't seem to have any control over his actions when she was near him.

He wiped the sweat from his forehead. When did he work that up? He'd been cold a minute ago. He stared out the window and saw a bush move. Instantly alert, he grabbed the Makarov from his waistband. Movement again. But this time the entire landscape seemed to sway. He blinked his eyes, his head swimming as he sank down onto the chair behind him.

Damn.

He wiped his forehead again then stood and scrutinized the front yard. All seemed still. He was just dizzy. Can't afford to get sick now. He went to the bathroom to wash his face in cold water, his lungs feeling heavy. Smoke inhalation sometimes didn't present symptoms until as much as twenty-four hours afterward. That's all he had, nothing more to it.

A bang next to him made him pick up his head. His gun had fallen to the floor. Had he dropped it? He opened the tap full strength and stuck his head under it.

"Are you okay?" Nicola stood in the doorway.

"ARE YOU OKAY?" she asked again, worried when he didn't respond. Was he ill?

He straightened and swayed.

She grabbed his arm. His skin was hot with fever. "Can you walk to the bed?"

He nodded and moved forward, leaning on her heavily. The trip to the pullout couch took several minutes.

She didn't have to tell him to lie down.

She rushed to the bathroom, closed the door and turned on the light. There had to be something in that kit that would help him. She rummaged through the dozens of bottles. Lucky for her, next to the pharmaceutical name, each label also contained a plain English description scribbled on by hand. She grabbed three—"fever," "pain" and "antibiotic"—then read the dosage.

She wet a towel before she shut off the light and went back to Alex. He would feel better soon. He had to. She draped the folded towel over his forehead and set the pills on the floor next to him until she got a glass of water. She took one pill from each bottle then held them out to him.

"Here, take these."

He did so before falling back on the pillow with a groan.

Stubborn, stubborn man. He should have gone to the hospital. She looked at Mrs. Slocsky's cell phone on the kitchen counter. The last person he had talked to was his boss. If she hit redial... She grabbed the phone and pushed the power button. The screen remained black. She pushed power a few more times before she realized the battery was dead.

Nicola sat on the edge of the bed, defeated and bone tired. Alex was out, she had no phone, and she had no idea where she was. He had taken back roads, different ones each time. A wave of panic pushed against her, threatening to drown her. She fought it. For herself and for Alex. He needed her. She would not let him down.

Help was on the way, she was sure of it. Alex had called. She wondered how her father fared, if he'd heard of this latest attack by now. Was he safe? Suddenly she would have given anything to know.

She rubbed her forehead, and her fingertips came away black. God, she was filthy. She rubbed at the dark spots on her leg and they smudged, not shadows after all, but soil and soot from climbing all over creation.

She had to take a shower. She had washed her hands before she treated Alex's wounds, but if she were to take care of him, the rest of her had better be clean, too. She didn't dare risk him getting an infection due to less than sanitary conditions.

She grabbed a long T-shirt from the hall closet, walked into the bathroom, then turned on the light and looked at herself in the mirror for the first time that night. She looked as if she'd been rolled in mud. Hard to believe Alex had actually kissed her like that. His mind must have been addled by pain. And, of course, it had been dark.

Shouldn't be thinking about his kisses. They were dangerous—gentle and passionate at the same time—the kind you wished went on and on, the kind that could make a woman fall in love with the man. And she couldn't do that. Not with Alex. He would be gone the day his assignment ended. And she was all stocked up in the heartbreak department already.

She took a deep breath, picked up the gun from the floor and set it on the edge of the sink, before taking off the Kevlar vest and chucking it into the corner. After she stripped out of her clothes, she washed them and hung them on the side of the shower glass, underwear included. In this heat, her panties and bra would be dry and back in place in no time.

Alex seemed to be sleeping by the time she was done with her shower and got back to him, wearing nothing but the long T-shirt, her hair wet. The towel had slipped from his forehead. She put it back on, her fingers brushing his skin in the process. He was burning up.

She went back into the bathroom and wet a few more towels. When she'd been little and had a bad fever, her mother used to wrap her entire body in a wet sheet. That had always worked. Clearly, Alex needed more than a piece of cloth on his forehead.

"Take your clothes off." She sat next to him.

He mumbled something undistinguishable.

She tried to lift his torso, but couldn't budge him beyond an inch or two. He was way too heavy for her.

"Alex, wake up."

His eyes fluttered open for a brief second, giving her hope, then closed again. He was completely out.

Fine. She would have to do what she could on her

own. Careful of his wounds, she tugged up his T-shirt as far as it would go without him sitting up. She rolled him on his left side and freed one arm, then rolled him on his right side and freed the other. Then finally she could pull the thing over his head.

The shirt out of the way, she moved on to the pants and had an easier time; his legs were not as heavy to lift. She wrapped one wet towel around his broad chest and one on each of his legs, then sat back with nothing more to do but worry.

She did a damned fine job of it, sitting on the sofa behind him, guarding his sleep. But more needed to be guarded than just his sleep. She needed to guard their lives. *The terrorists.* For the past hour she had forgotten about them. Not very smart. Nicola got up and retrieved his gun from the bathroom. It was up to her now to keep them safe.

She settled back on the sofa in a position from where she could see the door and the windows. Did the gun have a safety feature? Was it on? How would she take it off? All she knew about guns she had learned from the movies. God, she was pitiful. What did she hope to do if the terrorists came?

Snap out of it. She'd do what she had to. First she would have to stay alert so she would know if they were there. Then if she heard or saw anything suspicious, she would have to try to wake Alex. If that didn't work, she'd aim as best she could and squeeze the trigger. In a best-case scenario, some bullets would come out. Yes, that would definitely be a bonus.

"YOU MAKE YOUR ancestors proud, soldier." The General leaned back in his chair, enjoying the bit of good news. It wouldn't be long now.

"Thank you, General."

A trolley went by outside his window and he waited until the noise settled down. "All is prepared?"

"Yes, General."

His goal was so close he could almost taste success and the glory that would come with it. "Do whatever you have to. We cannot fail again. Time is running out."

"Everything is set up, General. This time she will have no escape."

No, she wouldn't. He had been right to come to America. This operation was too important for him not to be personally involved. As the old saying went, "If you don't go into the cave of the tiger, how are you to get its cub?"

Well, he was in the cave, and he would get the cub. And then he would face the tiger.

He closed his cell phone and took another look at the makeshift lab before he walked out. It had been a good day. One of his men had found Nicola. The

General nodded to the guard in the hall. Tso had accomplished the impossible. Not that he'd had any doubts. If anyone could pull this off it was Tso, one of the most eminent scientists in China, before word had gotten out that he was an anticommunist.

Everything was ready. He did not revel in the destruction to come, but neither did he fool himself into thinking there was any other way. Something large scale had to be done to get the world's attention, something despicable enough to make it impossible for the United States not to respond.

His people had tried for decades to rid themselves of tyranny, losing tens of thousands of lives in the process and getting no help from the "civilized" West, not even when masses of students lay dead on Tienanmen Square, massacred in front of the cameras.

Sons of Peace had been named in respect for those young men and women. Tienanmen—the Gate of Heavenly Peace. But the similarities ended there. Peaceful demonstrations didn't work, as had been amply demonstrated in 1989. The Sons of Peace, ironically, were proponents of war. And if the United States was unwilling to help when it was asked nicely, for fear of risking its lucrative trade relations, then the Sons of Peace were not afraid to force the hand of this mighty nation.

For the freedom of their country, the Sons of Peace

were more than willing to sacrifice a few U.S. senators, indeed even themselves.

HIS HEAD FELT GROGGY and he was lying down. Strange. Alex opened his eyes, then closed them against the bright sunlight that poured into the room. He distinctly remembered sitting guard by the window.

He opened his eyes again, just a slit this time. He was definitely on the pullout couch. He lay on his side facing the living room, a bunch of soggy towels on the bed in front of him. Other than his underwear, he was naked. When did that happen? He looked at the arm that was in pain. Freshly bandaged. Couldn't remember that, either.

Then he became aware of something else utterly unexpected and went still. Nicola was sleeping behind him, her face pressed against his naked back.

One confused emotion chased another in his head as he eased away from her and sat up. She looked exhausted but still beautiful. And dangerous. He took the Makarov from her, unable to resist brushing a few wayward curls from her face.

Had she stayed up all night to take care of him? Why couldn't he remember anything? The pain hadn't been that bad. He'd certainly lived through worse. His feet knocked over the answer on the floor—pill bottles. He picked up the culprit of his disoriented state. Algmir. A painkiller or, more specifically, a strong opiate given to soldiers in battle with critical injuries.

She had drugged him.

And in the process left herself defenseless for the entire night. He swore and chucked the bottle across the floor, madder at himself than at her, as he remembered how she'd put the pills into his mouth and told him to swallow. What the hell had he been thinking? He must have been out of it if he hadn't questioned her.

He stood and looked back at the woman on the bed who had managed to do what no enemy had ever accomplished—rendered him useless for hours in the middle of an operation. Had she realized the kind of danger she had put them in?

She lay on top of the covers in nothing but an oversize T-shirt, looking deceptively innocent. His mouth went dry. Probably from more than the aftereffects of the drugs. They were efficient, that was for sure. He was still pain free, but seemed to have trouble with basic motor skills. He was having the hardest time turning his head from Nicola.

She had taken off her vest.

Two emotions battled inside him for control: anger that she had drugged him, then discarded the only protection she had left; and gut-wrenching lust. The thin T-shirt showed every tempting line of those curves he had spent weeks fantasizing about.

She had legs to die for, buttocks and hips round enough to be inspirational, breasts that nearly made him cry with need. He had as much self-restraint as the next man, but he was rapidly reaching the end of it. God hadn't made this woman to be resisted. And yet he must. Alex turned on his heels and dragged himself off to the bathroom for a cold shower.

It didn't help. The second he stepped back into the living room, the stubborn erection he had sought to ease under the cold spray was back. He wasn't sure it would ever go away. They might have to bury him with it when he died.

Funny how that worked. Even after several hours of sleep, his body felt weak. Except for that one part.

He grabbed the cell phone and went outside to the car. A quick search turned up the cord that fit into the cigarette lighter for recharge. Alex left the barn door open while he ran the motor long enough to at least partially charge the battery. He had meant to do that last night, before he'd gotten drugged into oblivion.

When he went back inside, he sat by the window, not trusting himself near the bed.

He heard her stir, but forced himself not to turn

around. The bed creaked as she got out, as did the hardwood floor when she made her way to him.

"I'm glad you're feeling better." She hugged him from behind.

NICOLA FELT HIS MUSCLES stiffen and let him go. Maybe he didn't like her touching him. Although, he had seemed to like her well enough when he had kissed her last night. Twice.

He smelled like soap, his dark hair still wet from the shower. She glanced at his hands and neck. He had bandaged his burns.

"How are you doing?" She went to the kitchen and started breakfast. He needed to eat to replace the blood he had lost.

"Fine. Don't ever knock me out again."

"What?"

"The Algmir. You left us exposed."

Sheesh, he should be thanking her for making him feel better. He had needed rest. "I was handling security."

He made a rude sound. "You didn't wake up when I took the gun from you."

She fixed him with a stare. "Are we or are we not still alive?"

He had nothing to say to that.

She looked through the cabinets. The man needed a decent meal. Something to make him less grumpy.

Eggs and bacon and home fries. She opened a can of organic chunky potato soup with bacon, the closest thing they had, and dumped its contents into a pot to warm up on the stove.

He came over to sit at the table, gulped down the soup when it was ready, then ate a full MRE and downed two glasses of water. She cleaned up his mess.

"Thank you." He reached for her hand as she bustled around to keep busy.

The banked fire in his eyes awakened all her senses at once. She looked away, her gaze settling on the old scars below his elbow. Without thinking, she reached out to trace them with a finger. He didn't pull away this time.

"Chemical burns," he said with a matter-of-fact voice.

She waited for him to tell her more, not sure if he would.

"I was working on infiltrating a biochemical weapons factory overseas. Had inside help from one of the scientists forced to work there."

"What happened?"

"Somehow they caught on to him." He swallowed. "They asked him about me, and he refused to answer. They shot his wife in front of him."

"Oh my God."

"When he still didn't talk, they shot his son. With

guns to his daughter's head, he finally told them all he knew. It wasn't much, so they shot the daughter, too, then beheaded him in the town square for treason."

"Did they catch you?"

"Almost. They set a trap, but I managed to get away with only this." He pointed to his back, then didn't say anything more for a while.

"Abu was my friend. I talked him into cooperating. I had authorization to offer him and his family asylum as soon as the operation was over."

ALEX LOOKED UP and watched as tears filled her eyes. She rubbed them away, but more took their place, their flow unstoppable like soldiers spilling from their bunkers, rushing in each other's steps to battle.

The only other person he'd talked to about this was Colonel Wilson. Hard to believe the Colonel would trust him with Nicola, come to think of it, considering that the last man he'd worked with and his family were dead. Not exactly the right recommendation for a bodyguard.

But the Colonel did trust him to get the job done. Trouble was, Alex wasn't sure he trusted himself.

A fat tear rolled down Nicola's face. It touched him that she'd cry for Abu and his family, people she didn't even know.

"Oh, Alex. I'm so sorry. It must have been terrible

for you.'' She wiped the tears with the back of her hand.

She was crying for him? The thought was so unlikely, it took him a heartbeat or two to catch up with it.

She hadn't cried when people were shooting to kill her, when she'd had to take over the wheel in the middle of a high-speed chase, when her house was burning. But she cried for him.

He pulled her into his arms, and she buried her face against his shirt. He couldn't remember anyone ever crying for him before, caring enough to cry.

That's what did him in at the end—not her tantalizing curves or intoxicating allure, but her tears.

He kissed the soft curls on the top of her head, and when she looked up, he kissed away her tears. Then, while he was at it, he kissed her lips too, with military thoroughness.

No vest stood between them this time, and he could not keep his hands off her, exploring her voluptuous beauty, reveling in the full breasts that filled his palms to overflowing. When his thumbs found her nipples, she moaned into his mouth.

He felt much better—the result of having a good meal in his stomach and Nicola in his lap. The day was shaping up well. They were back in the safe house, and, considering last night's events, they would probably stay here for some time. The thought of extended inactivity didn't seem to bother him as much as it had in the past. He kissed her for all he was worth. Yeah, he could take a few days of this…

Or more.

No. Not more. He couldn't do more. He shouldn't even be doing what he was already doing. But, damn, it felt good. Even if they could go no further. Frustration might kill him, but having his lips on hers and his hands on her body were worth it.

Another minute and he would stop. He was responsible enough not to go too far. He was a trained military man with all kinds of discipline.

As if she had read his thoughts, she pulled away and stood. Too soon, but probably better that way. He came off the chair, too, wanting to get past the awkward moment when they would both mumble something idiotic then walk in opposite directions to pretend the last few minutes hadn't happened.

Instead Nicola looked into his eyes and said, "I want you so much, it drives me crazy."

Her words slammed into his chest with enough force to nearly knock him back onto the chair. Oh, hell. Feeling none of his injuries, he lifted her into his arms and walked to the bed.

Unable to take his lips from hers long enough to see what he was doing, he tumbled onto the sheets with her. She kissed him, holding nothing back, and helped him peel off her T-shirt, until her generous breasts spilled into the light for his hungry gaze. He buried his head between them, lost in the feeling of her velvet skin against his cheeks.

He tasted one then the other, going back and forth, a man with a new addiction. She was everything he had thought he would never have. A woman who was willing to accept the half answers he was able to give about his job, who could look at his scars and not turn away repulsed. Smart, beautiful, generous.

He had spent hours on end imagining her like this in his arms, and now that she was here, he had trouble believing it.

He trailed kisses down her belly, caressing her hips and lavishing her belly button. He was determined not to stop until he tasted every maddening curve. A man on a mission, his objective was clear: to make her blood rush as crazy with desire as she made his.

His path unobstructed by underwear, he moved lower and lower, aroused by her moans then satisfied by her sudden silence once he had leisurely sampled everything.

He came up next to her and kissed her swollen lips. Long moments later, he pulled back and tried to memorize her face the way she looked just now, flushed with desire, smiling, ready to give herself to him.

He moved back just enough to remove his clothes, then kissed her again as he positioned himself above her.

"Are you sure?" he murmured against her lips, knowing he'd die if she said no, yet still willing to stop.

She pushed him away enough to look him fully in the eyes. "I've never been more sure about anything."

He crushed her to him, ready to devour the mouth that had spilled those precious words. Positioned at her opening, he stopped, swore as he pulled away.

"What?" She tried to pull him back.

"Protection. We don't have any." He cursed himself and fell on his back on the bed next to her.

She turned to her side and watched him for an agonizing moment. "I'm not ovulating right now." Her cheeks flushed. "If that's what you're worried about."

She didn't know how much she tempted him.

"Oh," she said when he didn't respond. "I've only been with one man before. We always used protection."

He turned to look at her. The frustration in her eyes mirrored his own. Using protection was the only rule he'd never broken. Until now. "Me, too."

He groaned with need as she slid into his arms.

"So—" Nicola nibbled his ear. "Since we're in a safe house, does that mean this is safe sex?"

He couldn't help grinning at the pun. "Absolutely," he said, and claimed her lips.

By the time he entered her he was ready to burst at the sensation of her tight, hot muscles closing around him. He was going to shame himself climaxing way too soon. SDDU soldiers prided themselves on their stamina. He feared he wouldn't be able to show Nicola any of it. At least, not this time.

He waited unmoving, savoring the moment and the feel of her. Then he pushed forward inch by agonizing inch. She was wet for him, her sheath welcoming. She squirmed, nearly undoing the last of his self-control. He'd been wanting this from the first moment he'd seen her, fantasized about it during the endless nights of covert surveillance. And now they were here. Reality made his wildest fantasies pale in comparison.

Her skin looked like sweet cream in the moonlight, and he lapped it up. He kissed every inch available to his searching lips, his hips moving forward still. And then he was finally in all the way, completely surrounded.

She locked her feet around his back and drew him deeper. No military self-discipline training had prepared him for that. Nothing had ever felt so good.

They fit each other like two perfect halves of a whole, like she'd been meant to be his.

He drew a ragged breath as he began to move in her, each slow stroke the most exquisite torture. She moved with him, matching his rhythm at first, then taking over, dictating the speed. They came together faster and faster in a frenzied coupling, in runaway passion. He wasn't going to make it. Alex shuddered, then the next second felt her spasms, and finally he let go his release. The waves of pleasure seemed to go on and on, cresting deep inside his body.

She clung to him, as he did to her, unable to move.

Several minutes passed before he regained his bearings enough to roll off her and, still not ready to part, he pulled her with him.

Chapter Eight

"That thing you said about the one guy?" Alex asked a while later, when he could speak again.

"Does it bother you?" She came up on her elbows to look at him, so beautiful it took his breath away.

He grunted.

"Why?" Her breast brushed against his arm, stirring renewed interest in parts that by all rights should have been panting with exhaustion.

He could distinctly feel a nipple poke his skin. Damned hard to keep track of what they were talking about. The guy. Right.

"On the one hand, I want to track him down and kill him for touching you, on the other, I want to slap myself for taking advantage of a virtual innocent."

She smiled. "Would it help if I told you he never, um, made me happy…that way?"

"You mean you never had a—"

She shook her head.

Alex stared at her. ‘‘It doesn’t help. It just confuses the issue. Now I want to kill him for letting you waste your time with him. But then, he must have made me look good by comparison.’’ He looked at her from hooded eyelids, enjoying the smile that spread on her face.

‘‘Pretty damn good.’’

‘‘Great. Does that mean I…made you happy?’’

‘‘Very.’’ She snuggled up to him, the picture of contentment.

Very was good. He hoped she meant if she had climaxed any harder she would have needed medical attention. Like him. He closed his arms around her and held her tight. ‘‘My name is Alejandro Jesús Rodriguez,’’ he whispered into her hair.

She lifted her head to kiss his chin. ‘‘Thank you. I know you can’t tell me more than that.’’

And for the first time ever, he wanted to. He wanted one person outside the U.S. government to know him, to care whether he lived or died. ‘‘My mother died in Cuba when I was six. My father brought me to the U.S.’’

‘‘That must have been hard.’’

‘‘We didn’t speak English. He got a job on a farm where he thought that didn’t matter. But he had an accident. Didn’t understand the instructions and one of those big farm machines…’’ He hadn’t talked about it in years. Decades. Wasn't even sure what had happened. He'd been too young to understand.

Nicola tightened her arms around him.

"A family in Miami took me in after that. I joined the Army as soon as I was old enough. There had never been any possibility of having money for college. Made it to Special Forces. Later on, I got recruited for a project that was looking for high-performance loners for confidential operations with elevated risk levels."

She snuggled into the crook of his neck. "Thank you. But you didn't have to tell me."

"I wanted to." He kissed the top of her head, then her eyes, her cheeks, her lips, and she responded without holding back.

And once they started kissing, neither of them could stop. When they finally pulled apart, he propped himself on an elbow next to her to drink in the sight of her magnificent body.

"I worked with a Moroccan architect once," he told her. The man had provided him with blueprints to one of the key palaces in the region. "He used to say curved lines stimulated creativity. Must be something to it. I'm feeling extraordinarily creative."

He showed her what he meant until they were depleted from lovemaking once again. This time he made love to her slowly, building her passion touch by touch, kiss by kiss, pushing her over the edge again and again.

When the phone rang, he swore, tempted to ignore it. Of course, he couldn't. Not when Nicola's life might depend on whatever information the Colonel had.

"Rodriguez."

"Spike's on his way over there. He should be showing up in another ten or twenty minutes," the Colonel said.

"Anything new on the case?"

"No, but we're tightening security, both around the senator and his daughter. The FBI assigned three bodyguards to each, plus I'm leaving Spike with Nicola. She seems to be the primary target for now. We're leaving her where she is. Probably less risky than getting her out into the open while trying to move her down here."

"Spike's taking over?"

"You're shipping out tonight. Come see me as soon as you're done briefing him and we'll discuss it."

He swallowed, looking at Nicola on the bed, smiling at him so full of trust, her heart on her nonexistent sleeve. Like it or not, by making love to her, he had compromised the whole operation. Would he have recognized an enemy soldier at the window while he was lost in the pleasures of her body? He had allowed himself to be distracted, and that could have cost both their lives. He didn't much care about his own, but he did care about Nicola's.

She was better off with guards who were focused on protecting her instead of getting her between the sheets.

"See you tonight then," he said, and hung up the phone.

"Is Spike coming?"

"He's taking over the operation. Three FBI agents are also assigned to you now. They should be arriving later."

"And you?"

"I'll probably be shipping out overseas after my briefing tonight."

"I see." Her face went pale.

He hated this, but it had to be done. "Nicola, look, I…this is what my life is like."

"Of course." She wrapped the sheet around her and scooted off the bed. "I understand." She headed for the bathroom, walking around him.

"Don't be mad."

"I'm not mad." Her voice sounded lifeless. "I just want to get dressed before Spike gets here."

He couldn't stand the dejected set of her shoulders, and before he knew what he was doing, he had closed the distance between them and pulled her into his arms. "Look, it's better for you this way. You need bodyguards who are not personally involved."

He couldn't not think of Abu and his family. Technically his mission hadn't included their protection, but he felt responsible for them. He should have been able to save them. But it wasn't too late for Nicola, and he would make damned sure she got the best security detail available.

"Do I get a vote in what's best for me?" She looked up and his gut tightened at the sight of the teardrop in the corner of her eye.

He shook his head. "I'm sorry. Not this time."

"I see," she said again, pulling away.

"I promise I will find you when I come back." Although, he could not promise when that would be, a month from now or six, or a year. Maybe more. Maybe never. And the scary thing was this time he really wanted to come back. It mattered.

"I didn't plan this." He tried to take her hand, but she wouldn't let him.

"It's okay, Alex. It really is." She turned and walked into the bathroom.

He stared at the closed door, knowing it wasn't okay at all, but powerless to do anything about it. He had nothing whatsoever to offer her. He didn't even exist. He owned no property, although he could certainly afford it, but his brief visits to the States were usually spent at an army base near Washington, the fewer hassles the better. Even his car and gun weren't his own—they were issued by the SDDU, and now that they were destroyed, he'd be issued another set. His time wasn't his own, either, nor was his life. He had pledged it to the government of the United States of America, a decision he'd never second-guessed...until now.

He would hand her over to Spike because he trusted the man, because Nicola was better off without him, because his country needed him somewhere else. All perfectly valid reasons, yet they failed to satisfy him.

NICOLA WASHED HER FACE in cold water, then pressed her fingers to her eyelids to hold back the tears. She hadn't expected this. Then again, from the moment he had burst into her life to save her from a hail of bullets, nothing about Alex had been predictable.

A week ago he'd been nothing but the male lead in a fuzzy fantasy she'd concocted about a gorgeous guy at the gym. Then the world had turned upside down and her life had become unrecognizable. And the only reason she still had her life was the man in the living room, the man who had just made incredible love to her—twice—and was now planning to leave her.

She dressed, grateful that she'd had the state of

mind to wash her underwear the night before. Hopefully, Spike would bring her more.

If her house still stood.

The thought knocked the air out of her lungs for a moment. What had become of the Tweedles? She felt an overpowering rush of guilt for leaving them. What had become of her world? She had worked so hard to create a life separate from the political madness of her father's.

And now her pets were God only knew where, her house probably gone, including her home office with all her business documents. She would need months to recover, to be fully operational, and that was after Alex's boss—whoever the man was—decided to let her resume her life and leave here. Where would her clients be by then? Not a hard question to answer. They'd be with the competition.

Everything she'd ever worked for was gone—and all because of what? Because her father had stepped on some toes in China while carrying out orders from the government. It had nothing to do with her! How much more would she have to unwillingly give?

One thing for sure, if she wanted to separate her life from the intrigues of politics and government, getting involved with an undercover agent was not the way to go. God, what had she been thinking? Having her life stolen was enough, she wasn't going to offer up her heart to be broken, as well.

Alex was right. She'd be better off when he left.

Voices filtered through the door. Spike must have arrived. Nicola brushed her teeth, then ran the comb through her hair. The voices rose.

"Damn it, Alex. You should have told the Colonel you were injured. You're not out in the field where nothing can be done."

"I'm fine."

"No, you're not. You should be at Walter Reed and not in a high-risk operation where being less than one hundred percent could get you into serious trouble."

"It wasn't a high-risk operation until yesterday."

"It is now. You're to report to Washington posthaste for your briefing."

A moment of silence passed before Alex spoke. "What did you get from the shooter?"

"Not much. He stuck to his story about the family vendetta until I questioned him on the new attack. He's been quiet since. There's someone out there he's more afraid of than us."

"Any connection to Du Shaozu?"

"None. He's a legit businessman. Believe me I had him checked thoroughly."

"I still don't like him."

"Want me to give you a couple of guesses why?"

"Shut up." Nicola heard Alex's annoyed response through the door.

Had Spike picked up on the vibes between her and Alex? Better go out there before they decided to discuss her. She glanced briefly in the mirror—looking as bad as she felt and with no makeup to disguise the dark circles beneath her eyes. But under the circumstances, her appearance was the least of her worries. She turned off the light and opened the door.

Spike leaned against the counter while Alex hulked by the window, their conversation halted the second she appeared.

"Hello, Nicola." Spike turned to her with a smile. "How are you?"

"Okay, all things considered." She looked at the towel-covered cage next to the bulging duffel bag at Spike's feet, her hopes rising. "Have you been to my house?"

He nodded. "The birds are fine. The garage is a mess, though. The rest is still standing but there's considerable smoke damage. I got you some standard-issue military clothes. Sorry. That's the best I could do."

"Thank you." She pulled the towel from the cage, wanting to kiss the finches in joy when they immediately started their bickering.

"I need to grab a few more things from the car. My new car, since someone let my old one get destroyed." Spike gave Alex a pointed look. "Once Alex goes, I don't want to have to leave the house until the Feds get here,'' he said before walking out the door.

''Maybe I should stay.'' Alex stepped toward her.

She couldn't let him. He had to go to Washington where his colonel would make sure he got medical care. He had to leave before she made an even bigger mess of her life and fell in love with him.

''Have you ever done something in the heat of the moment, then regretted it once you had time to think?''

His sharp gaze cut to her soul. ''More times than I care to remember.''

''I think you should leave. I'd prefer it if you did.''

''Here we go, that'll be the last of it.'' Spike came through the door with two more duffel bags.

Alex looked at Nicola, his dark eyes unreadable. ''I'll be going, then.'' He picked up Mrs. Slocsky's car keys from the counter. ''Best of luck to both of you.''

He was out the door before she could say thank you.

She busied herself in the kitchen to keep from running to the window when she heard the car pull away. Not until the noise of the motor faded into the distance did she realize this was probably the last time she would ever see him.

Her hands stilled in the sink. The cup she'd been washing slipped from her fingers. She was incapable of doing anything but stare at the suds as they popped on the surface of the water, a terrible ache spreading in her chest.

The breeze outside brushed some of the tall weeds against the living room window, startling her. The sky looked overcast. Rain was coming. That uneasy feeling she had experienced the first time she'd seen the house settled on her again.

"How is my father handling all this?"

Spike looked up from checking one of Alex's sensors. "Fine. He's got an excellent security detail. No attempts on him so far. His biggest worry seems to be you. The only reason he's not here is because we wouldn't tell him where you were."

That surprised her. Other than insisting that she'd attend all major political functions with him, he hadn't paid much attention to her since her mother's death. She'd gone along with that for a while, craving his attention, glad for his company any way she could get it. But then she'd grown up and moved away. They hadn't attended a reception together in ages.

She was fine without him. She had other things in her life. Better things. The current mess she was in was all because of him.

Nicola looked at the clock on the oven: 9:00 a.m. A few more hours and the Feds would be here. She shut off the water and went to find her Kevlar vest.

She was probably safer now than she'd been since the whole ordeal had started. At least now they knew what they were up against. She had Spike by her side and more bodyguards on the way, and yet with Alex gone she felt as if her sense of security had also gone with him.

There wasn't any logic in that whatsoever. She had gotten used to Alex, and it would take time before she felt as comfortable around Spike, that was all. The pain in her chest was nothing but a lingering effect of smoke inhalation. She refused to consider any other possibility.

"Everything looks good." Spike finished his inspection. "I'm just gonna check in with the Colonel to tell him Alex is on his way, then nothing left to do but to wait. Do you play poker?" He pulled a pack of cards from an outer pocket of the duffel bag at his feet with a smile. "I thought it would help us kill some time."

She smiled back at him. Spike was all right. He had an easygoing manner, none of the dark looks and hard silences Alex wore like an ever-present cloak.

She missed Alex.

Better get used to it. She was unlikely to ever see him again. The pain in her chest deepened. She refused to play the "what if" game. She had to be honest with herself. Just as Alex had been. He'd never pretended to be anyone other than who he was.

They shared a morning of glorious lovemaking. She couldn't have more of him than that. She was mature enough to understand it.

"Poker sounds great," she said, then headed to the bathroom to throw some more cold water on her face to stop the tears that threatened to spill from her eyes.

She barely closed the door when a deafening explosion shook the house and nearly knocked her off her feet. She tried to open the door, had to shove hard as it seemed blocked.

"Spike?" she yelled, but could barely hear her own voice from the ringing in her ears. No response. Fear gave her strength. She pushed harder.

When she finally managed to get out, she could see little else than smoke, fire, dust and rubble everywhere.

They had come for her, and Alex wasn't here.

"Spike?" she shouted over the security alarm as she climbed over what had once been a coffee table to get out of the bathroom.

She saw movement by the window and stepped toward it on shaky legs. Spike peered through the dust and smoke. No, not Spike she realized too late as the masked man started for her. Another figure climbed in behind him. And another...and another.

Panic squeezed her chest as she scrambled back, choking on the air, and headed for the staircase. She locked the steel reinforced door behind her and looked around for somewhere to hide, or a way to get out. Through the holes in the roof, she could see the sky growing dark with storm clouds. She darted from one dilapidated room to the next, all empty with large gaps in the walls. Nowhere to hide there.

Somebody was banging against the door. She glanced at the window at the end of the hallway. The steel door would hold up to bullets, but her pursuers had explosives and she doubted it would be long before they used them.

She struggled with the window, stuck from years of neglect. She had to get out, then go back in downstairs to find Spike. He might be injured, and if he wasn't, they'd be better off fighting together. The door flew open with a loud bang behind her just as the window finally opened. She had barely enough time to look before she jumped.

Her fall was broken by the unkempt rhododendron bushes enough so she didn't break her neck, but still got badly scraped and bruised. *Get up,* her mother's voice said in her head. She couldn't. She lay on her side for a second, her shoulder drenched in pulsing pain, the air knocked out of her.

Two masked men ran toward her, and she scrambled to get away. If she could get as far as the cornfield— They reached her before she got around the corner. The first one threw himself at her and knocked her to the ground. She bit, scratched and kicked, nearly managing to get him off. Then he grabbed her necklace from behind and pulled hard. She struggled for air.

The second stood over them, his gun aimed at her head, yelling at her in Chinese to stop.

She swore at him and kicked his partner full strength where it counted. He jerked up, the clasp broke, and she could breathe again. The man rolled off her and she got up on her knees, ignoring the gun at her head. If he was going to kill her, then let him get it over with. She was determined to go out fighting.

Her gaze met his as she began to rise. Then he turned his gun around and slammed the butt into her temple. The pain was intense but only for a moment. Then darkness came and she felt nothing.

ALEX STARED into the retina scanner at the gate, then pulled into the parking lot once it identified him and authorized entrance.

He got out of the car and walked to the door, doing his best to fight off the sense of foreboding that had settled into his bones during his two-hour drive to Washington. He didn't feel right, and it was more than the pain of his burns or the deep throbbing in his shoulder. They were probably no worse than before, just seemed like that because he didn't have anything else to focus on. The farther he'd gotten from the safe house the worse he felt.

Better concentrate on how he would handle Colonel Wilson. He reached the door and stopped for another retina scan then walked in, nodding to the security guards who knew him by sight.

First off, he would refuse to go to the hospital. He was doing fine, the pain was bearable, and he preferred it by far to the prison of inactivity. Secondly, he would ask to be kept on the Barrington case. He had decided that on the way down. Whether Nicola wanted him there or not, he wanted to see the case to the end, until she was safe. He could always provide covert protection if that was the only way, without her ever knowing. At least he would get to see her again.

He took the staircase up to the fourth floor out of habit. He didn't like elevators. They were too easy to get trapped in—a particular incident in Belize came to mind. The Colonel's office was next to last on the left side of the hallway.

"Hello, Sylvia." He walked into the spacious room decorated with antique maps of the world, one of Colonel Wilson's weaknesses.

The Colonel's secretary, an ex-Marine in her forties with a hell of a figure and a tougher-than-steel attitude, looked up at him with a smile. "Good to see you, Alex. What happened to your arm?'' She came out of her seat to get a better look.

He had figured she would know. Spike must have called to check in by now.

''A minor accident,'' he said, grateful for Spike's discretion. It'd be easier to play it down and convince the Colonel he was good to go back, if the man hadn't already made up his mind.

''Can I see the Colonel?'' He knew better than to barge by her. Sylvia protected the office like a lady dragon protected her lair; the Glock on her side gave fair warning to anyone who was smart enough to pay attention. And Alex liked to think he was smart enough, especially after the tales he had heard of her tackling new recruits now and then who misunderstood the power structure in the front office.

He could have probably taken Sylvia in hand-to-hand combat, but didn't think the Colonel would appreciate him rolling around on the carpet with her. Colonel Wilson was as protective of his secretary as she was of him. One could say she was another of his weaknesses. Sometimes Alex wondered how long it would take before the man realized it.

''Sorry, Alex.'' She went back to her seat. ''He just got called over to the DHS. I have no idea when he'll return. You're welcome to wait.''

Alex nodded. The Colonel reported straight to the Homeland Security Secretary.

"Thanks, but I might as well go and take care of a couple of things, then come back. Thompson checked in lately?"

"Heard you were working the same case. He called in about half an hour ago from the Hill. Not much going on there. He's been sitting outside the senator's office all morning."

"Thanks, Sylvia. I'll be back in an hour or so. Can I leave this with you?" He gave her his broken cell phone. "I don't know if it can be fixed."

"No problem. I'll have a new one for you by the time you get back."

He left, glad for the extra time. Something didn't add up in this case. He was missing a piece of the puzzle. And he had a strong suspicion he knew who held it.

Time to see the senator.

"I TOLD HER TO STAY in Washington. Offered to pay for her security." Senator Barrington shook his graying head as he sat in his burgundy-leather executive chair in his Capitol Hill office.

If he hadn't known the man was related to Nicola, Alex wouldn't have been able to guess it. They didn't look alike. She was all soft curves while he had so many angles he could have been drawn with Etch A Sketch.

"She's safe now." Alex took in the man's surroundings that spoke of success and old money. "Is there anything else about your time in China you might not have remembered until now? Even if it seems insignificant. Anyone you think might be in a position to set up something drastic like this?"

Barrington shook his head again. "I already told everything to you people. My contacts were mainly with other diplomats, government officials. I had to deliver a lot of bad news, but I don't see how anyone could hold that against me. I was a representative of the United States. I didn't make those decisions, I merely conveyed them."

"The attacks seem personal. It appears they're targeting your daughter, rather than you. Do you have any idea why?"

"Probably because I always had fairly good security. They couldn't hurt me, so they decided to get to me through her?" He rubbed his forehead.

Not likely. If they wanted to get the senator, they would have found a way. "Can you think of any reason why someone would want to go after you that bad?"

He looked down, his angular face pale with exhaustion. "No."

"Are you sure?"

"Stop badgering me, I already told you everything I could." He stood, his frustration showing in his sudden choppy movements.

He was clearly agitated and worried enough already, but Alex couldn't leave Barrington alone no matter how much the man wished it. Not yet. Not until he had some answers. ''With all due respect, Senator, your daughter's life is at stake.''

The lines on his face seemed to deepen while he collected himself. ''I thought you were providing her with sufficient protection so we didn't have to worry about her life.''

''We are. But as it is, we can only get these terrorists if and when they make their next attempt. If we knew who they were, we could track them down and take them out of the picture long before they got anywhere near Nicola.''

The man sank back into his seat. ''I hate this.''

''I'm sure it's very stressful for you, sir.''

''There was a man in China...'' He turned to the window, but stared into the air instead of looking out.

''Yes?''

''General Meng.''

''Did you have any problems with him?''

''No, no problems. At one point the embassy was trying to reach out to various Chinese leaders to improve relations. He was invited to a few of those fancy receptions and we talked some. He had a daughter Nicola's age and the girls hit it off. Sort of became friends. I suppose Nicola must have been lonely.''

''Did you have an argument with the General?''

''On the contrary. He was a rather nice fellow. We had some good talks. He was a very influential man within the army, who very much supported his country's growth.''

''What kind of growth?''

''Toward democracy.''

That couldn't have gone down well with his superiors. ''What happened?''

''I encouraged him, of course. Change had been our hope for that country for decades. Unfortunately, he took my enthusiasm literally as U.S. support and ended up involved in some rather unfortunate business.''

Alex leaned forward in his chair, hoping for a clue to follow.

''He spoke up openly for democracy and was of course severely ostracized. He thought with the Chinese army and the United States behind him, he could make certain things happen, but he was wrong on both counts.''

The senator got out of his chair, then sat back down again, as if at a loss as to what to do. ''He was thrown into prison. His soldiers followed their new general, and the U.S. decided not to risk diplomatic relations by making an issue out of the incident.'' He rubbed his forehead again. ''He died in prison. Very unfortunate. I came back to the States not long after that.''

Alex stood, ready to go. He'd had high hopes for the General, but the man was dead. His answer must come from somewhere else.

''Did he have a son?'' He asked from the door. You could never discount familial loyalty when it came to revenge.

''Just the daughter.''

''Thank you for taking the time to talk to me.''

''No problem.'' The senator seemed to have shrunken in his chair. ''I wish I could have helped more. How is Nicola holding up?''

''Very well, sir. She's a brave young woman.''

''Is she? I know her so little. Should have insisted on more security for her from the beginning. I didn't think she'd agree to it, you know. I was sure if I forced it on her she'd do whatever she could to dodge the guards. She did that in China once. Sneaked out of the embassy and gave her mother and me a fright. She never liked what I did for a living.''

Alex remained silent. It wasn't his place to comment.

The senator looked him straight in the eye. ''Take

good care of her. Whatever else happens, she must be safe."

"Yes, sir," he said before he left.

THE DRIVE BACK to SDDU headquarters took less than thirty minutes.

Sylvia looked up and smiled as Alex entered the door. "Go right in, the Colonel is waiting for you."

"Sylvia says you're injured." Colonel Wilson, a man sporting plenty of battle scars of his own, came to his feet to greet Alex as soon as he walked in.

Alex closed the door behind him. He should have put on a turtleneck before coming to Washington. Then again, in the middle of July, that would probably have aroused suspicion. Who was he kidding, no matter what he did, there would have been no escaping Colonel Wilson. "Nothing serious."

"I'll just wait on the official medical opinion on that."

"No time."

"You won't be shipping out until tonight."

"About that, I was wondering if I could ask a favor."

"Anything. God knows I owe you a few."

"You don't owe me anything, Colonel, but I'd appreciate this just the same. It's about the Barrington case."

"Spike has it in hand, I trust."

"Yeah, but something doesn't add up. First they

tried to shoot her, then the fire. I've been wondering..."

"I trust your judgment, Alex. If you have any ideas I want to hear them."

"Something seems off with the attacks. Like this last one."

"Lucky they didn't have a bomb."

"Exactly. At first I thought they just wanted to create a diversion, something to make us come running outside where they could gun her down. They had a lot of men waiting for us."

The Colonel nodded. "One good sniper could have done the job."

"And back to the bomb issue," Alex went on. "Why didn't they use one? If all they wanted was to kill her? Why start a fire in the garage instead of setting off a bomb in the house?"

"You don't think they want to kill her?"

"No, sir. Now that I have had time to consider it, I think they want to kidnap her."

"But then why shoot at her at the market?"

"Spike told me all the bullets were high, way off. What if they shot up the place to make sure everyone kept down and no one interfered when they tried to grab her?"

"A kidnapping for what purpose?"

"I don't know yet. To blackmail her father for money perhaps? To make him vote their way in some issue important to them?" Alex shrugged, frustrated by too many unanswered questions.

The Colonel narrowed his eyes as he considered this theory. He grabbed the phone and dialed, waited for a while then hung up.

"Spike's cell is out of service." His expression turned serious.

Alex's heart jumped. "Are the Feds there yet?"

"Haven't even left."

"I'm going back."

The Colonel nodded. "Head over to FBI headquarters. I'll call ahead and get you a chopper and as many men as I can."

"Thanks. One more thing. Could you check on what we have on a General Meng and his daughter?"

"No problem. Take care of yourself, Alex."

Sylvia looked up when he walked out of the Colonel's office. "Your new phone just got dropped off." She handed him a brand-new cell phone. "They were able to recover the chip from the old one, so it's loaded the same. All your information is still in there."

"Thanks, Sylvia. You're the best." He clipped the phone on his belt, then took off to find Nicola.

Chapter Nine

Nicola opened her eyes, struggling with the buzz of pain in her head. Alex. She could have sworn she'd heard him talking to her. She peered around in the semidarkness. Must have dreamt his voice. She was definitely alone.

Stone walls, solid-looking oak door, a lightbulb hanging from a wire overhead. She was in some kind of a basement, the air cold and dank, the smell of mold permeating the small room. She shivered, wanting to wrap her arms around herself but couldn't. They were tied behind her back.

Her head throbbed as she turned and focused on the small window behind her, too high to see anything. Still daylight though, that much she could tell. How long had she been out? She squirmed on the chair she was tied to, the only piece of furniture in the barren room. The ropes held tight.

From the fact that they hadn't gagged her, it was

safe to assume they weren't worried about her calling for help. No sense wasting her breath trying it. And if she didn't make too much noise, maybe her captors wouldn't realize for a while that she was awake, which could give her precious time to plan her escape.

She tested the ropes again. Only her wrists were tied, linked together around the back of the chair. She slid her hands a few inches up and down. They moved freely. She wasn't tied to the chair, thank God. They had been either careless or confident that she wouldn't be able to escape from the room.

If Alex were here, he'd find a way out.

Nicola struggled to stand, dragging the chair with her, shaking it to get loose. She felt her hands slide up on the back an inch or so, then a little more. She wiggled her shoulders from side to side until the chair finally fell away with a loud crash.

Had they heard her? She leaned against the cold wall, her knees stiff. She waited a minute, then two. Nobody came.

She walked to the window, a good three feet above her head, and stared out at the cloudless sky. It was the only thing she could see from that angle. Some time had apparently passed since she'd been taken. She remembered the dark sky at the safe house and the storm about to break.

She sat on the floor and curled into as tight a ball

as she could, the flexibility gained by all those years of Tai Chi coming in handy now. Little by little she worked her hands over her legs to the front then took a good look at the rope.

Thin but sturdy, and tied tight. She twisted her wrists but could not get out. She lowered her head and sank her teeth into the knot, ignoring the foul taste, then began to work herself free.

It felt like a long time before she got the rope loose, her jaw aching from the effort. She rubbed her sore wrists as she stood and looked at the window again.

She jumped. Not high enough. She jumped again. This time the tips of her fingers touched the sill, but she couldn't get a good grip and slid down. On the third try she finally managed to hold on and pull herself up long enough to take a peek outside before she fell back once again.

The window looked out to the inner courtyard of a Chinese-style building, complete with pagoda roofs. On the next jump she tested the large padlock that held the window closed. It was as sturdy as it looked.

Nicola paced the room, going around the chair that lay on its side. The chair. Right. She could have gotten up on that instead of all the jumping. Why hadn't she thought of that? Because she was too panicked to think. Whoever had dumped her in this basement had some kind of plans for her, plans she was certain she wasn't going to like.

She carried the chair to the window and climbed up to examine the padlock again, pulled on it, rattled it to no avail—securely locked. She couldn't go through there.

She stepped off the chair and sat down. Now what? Her gaze fell on the door. Could it be that simple? She got up to try. Nope, the door was locked, as well, the wood old but thick. She didn't even bother to try to kick it open. From what she could see, she doubted a rhinoceros could get through those panels held together by ornate wrought-iron braces.

But if she couldn't break down the door, could she break the window? She turned over the chair and worked one of its legs loose. She set the three-legged leftover next to the wall, and balancing carefully, stood on it to look outside. The courtyard was empty. But even if the kidnappers were indoors, they would probably hear the breaking glass. She would have to be quick.

She took a deep breath and smashed the chair leg against the glass, working as fast as she could, careful to get all the shards out of the frame. It would be a tight fit.

She was done in less than a minute, then used the piece of wood to brush the broken glass off the inside sill. Couldn't do much about the shards that fell outside and now covered the brick pavers in front of her window. She needed something to protect her hands. Nicola glanced around the room, but didn't find anything suitable. And she had nothing but…the clothes on her back. Right.

A tank top, shorts, bra, and panties. No time to waste on being shy. She pulled her clothes off, set her underwear aside, then put the shorts and tank top back on before she wrapped her panties around her left hand, her bra around the right, wishing she wore the padded kind. Unfortunately, she'd never needed extra padding anywhere. Until now.

She climbed up on the chair, grabbed on to the window frame and pulled, then stepped on the back of the wobbly chair to give herself more leverage. Then her head was out, her chest, the broken glass crunching under her. She couldn't afford to think about that now. If she didn't hurry she was likely to end up with much graver injuries from whoever had kidnapped her.

She pulled herself through the window inch by inch, barely taking time to catch her breath once she was fully out. She brushed the shards off her skin and took a look at the cuts. The bottom of her arms were the worst, elbow to wrist, and then her knees. No major gashes but plenty of smaller cuts. But she had more important things to worry about. Nicola glanced around the deserted courtyard and scooted along next to the wall in a crouch.

An open gate stood not a hundred feet from her. An eternity passed before she made it there. She peered out from behind one of the wooden columns flanking the gate, not wanting to run into her captors on the other side. No terrorists were there, but neither was her freedom. She stepped into a small walled-in garden. She could hear the noises of a street outside the walls—cars, people talking.

In Chinese.

Was she in China? They couldn't have possibly smuggled her out of the country, could they? She broke out in a cold sweat at the thought.

"Hot dogs. Two dollars apiece with fixings," a deep voice called from somewhere on the other side.

She relaxed enough to be able to breathe again. Chinatown? But where? Philadelphia? She didn't dare call attention to herself by shouting to the passersby on the other side of the wall.

She crouched behind a bush, took the underwear off her hands and shook the remaining bits of glass out. After dabbing the cloth at the blood on her arms and legs, she stuffed the soiled pieces into her shorts pockets. If Alex could handle his burns and getting shot, she could handle a few scratches. Had she not insisted that he go away, she probably wouldn't be in this trouble now. Alex had promised he wouldn't let anything happen to her as long as she was under his protection.

She believed him.

The wall stood about eight feet high, and she could see nothing to step on. She looked around the perimeter for a suitable tree until she found one tall enough and close enough to the wall. She had climbed a tree before. *Once.* And technically she hadn't climbed it. Alex had pushed her up. But still, it had been nighttime and a house fire was burning under her. If she could manage under those circumstances, she should be able to manage now. She sure wasn't going to give up without trying.

She grabbed on to the lowest branch of the sizable dogwood and, supporting herself with her feet on the trunk, pulled herself up. People were shouting in the courtyard behind her, the sound of boots running on stone echoed between the walls. She stood on shaky knees and grabbed for the next branch.

Too late. Men came running into the garden. Rifles pointed at her from every direction.

She let go of the branch and slid to the ground, but sprung up immediately to dash between the men.

One of them stepped forward to block her way and shoved her to the ground. When she got up, he slapped her hard across the face, then grabbed her arm to drag her behind him. She ignored the taste of blood and gave him no further trouble, not wanting to provoke them. Her goal was to stay alive long enough to make another attempt to regain her freedom.

She made sure to notice every detail—the door, the corridors and the rooms that opened from it, as well as the staircase that led downstairs. They took her back into the basement. She could see the feet of the guard posted in front of her window. She huddled on the floor in the corner—someone had taken the broken chair—and was grateful they didn't tie her up. She tried desperately to think of a new plan, anything that had even the slightest chance of working. Unfortunately, she didn't have sufficient time to come up with a workable idea.

Not long after the soldiers left, an old man came to see her. He wore the same black paramilitary uniform as the others, but without the face mask. Cold brown eyes examined her from below his thinning gray hair. The man's gaze swept over her, hesitating on her injuries.

He began to speak, a lengthy apology in Mandarin. She blinked several times as if confused, not wanting to let him know she understood. She needed every advantage she could get.

He switched to accented English. "Sorry my men too rough. They used to battlefields not pretty women."

She finally recognized him, so shocked it took several seconds before she found her voice. "General Meng. What happened to you?"

The man in front of her was but a shadow of the respected general she had known in China. His fingers were gnarled, his hair completely gray and thinning, and scars, old ones, dotted his hands and face.

Although she had asked him in English, he responded in Chinese, pleasantries about how good it was to see her again. She looked suitably bewildered, not too hard under the circumstances, and pretended not to understand a solitary word.

"You forgot, then?" he finally asked in English with a small smile, a mad light burning in his eyes.

"I could barely grasp the basics even when we lived there." How true that was. She had often driven Mei, the General's daughter, crazy with frustration when her friend had tried to teach her some elementary Mandarin after school. She spoke it almost fluently now, thanks to the Chinese language minor she had chosen at Bryn Mawr.

She had wanted to tell Mei about her newfound proficiency, share how her life had turned out, but her best friend in China hadn't responded to her letters so she had given up on contacting her years ago. Seeing Mei's father now was beyond strange.

Had they moved to the States? What did he have to do with the kidnapping? Was he here to rescue her? Probably not, as nice as that would have been.

He had called the soldiers his men. Dozens of questions flew through her head.

She voiced the first. "Where is Mei?"

The man's face hardened. He lifted a hand and she thought he might hit her, but he merely rubbed his right temple instead. His gaze wandered around the room before settling on the guard outside the window. When he finally looked back at her it was with mild surprise, as if he'd forgotten she was there.

"I will send food and clothes. You rest. Tomorrow will be big day." He left without giving her a chance to find out anything more.

Stunned, Nicola sat on the cold, hard floor, a flock of thoughts chasing each other in her head, each more bizarre than the one that came before it. Then she heard the key turn in the lock. That at least told her something. General Meng or not, she was still a prisoner. But for what purpose? What were the General and his men planning to do with her?

ALEX LOOKED at the small glistening lake below as they flew over Maryland, fear for Nicola ripping through him. He had tried to reach her a couple of times, but she hadn't responded. It didn't mean anything, he told himself. She probably took the earpiece out and the necklace off after he'd left, thinking they'd be no use since they were programmed to his broken phone. His new cell phone buzzed and he grabbed it, disappointed when he saw the regular incoming call. He plugged the phone into his headset.

"We might have something with General Meng." The chopper's rotor blades nearly drowned out the Colonel's voice. "He attempted to start an uprising during Barrington's last year as U.S. ambassador there. Got thrown into jail and badly tortured. His property had been confiscated by the government, his wife and daughter beaten and raped by some communist commando. The wife died, the daughter committed suicide later."

Yeah, Alex thought. That would be enough to piss anyone off. "Barrington said he was dead."

"About Barrington," the Colonel went on. "It looks like he might have encouraged General Meng, but then the U.S. didn't follow up. Prison records show the General died in his cell, but according to our sources he escaped a little over two years ago."

The short hairs stood up on the back of Alex's neck. In his line of work he had to rely on intuition frequently, and he had learned to trust his. It was now sounding the high alarm. "Anything else?"

"One of his old friends was arrested last year in connection with an antigovernment paramilitary group, Sons of Peace. They were planning a major attack against key members of the party. We're looking into that, trying to find a U.S. connection."

"Thanks for letting me know, Colonel."

Alex clicked off and turned his attention back to the ground below. They had crossed into Pennsylvania. As the chopper flew over sprawling acres of farmland, he could make out several Amish buggies mixed in with cars on the roads.

"There." He spotted the safe house and pointed it out to the pilot.

The front window was missing.

He leaned forward in his seat, his muscles tense, his chest as tight as if a camel had sat on him. He blinked to clear his eyes, willing the picture to go away, but saw more bad news instead as the pilot circled the house. Debris littered the backyard, the sight making his throat go dry and his palms sweat.

No wonder the Colonel hadn't been able to reach Spike. Judging from the wreckage below, the terrorists hadn't messed around this time. They'd blown up the middle of the house, the kitchen and living room where Nicola and Spike were most likely to have been.

Maybe his theory on them wanting to kidnap Nicola had been wrong. From this vantage point, it sure looked like they had gone for a direct kill. And if so, it wasn't likely they had left without making sure they had achieved their mission.

He was too late.

The thought squeezed the last of the air out of his lungs and he fought to breathe, to grab some oxygen in hoarse gasps, refusing to consider the pictures that tried to invade his brain—Nicola's broken body in the wreckage below. And Spike…

He hung on as the pilot set the chopper down in the tall grass behind the house and was out and running toward the building before the motor was off.

The agents scrambled to provide him cover, but he ignored their shouts to stop and wait.

"Nicola! Spike!" He climbed through the rubble in the living room, not really expecting anyone to answer. Whoever had done this did a thorough job.

He heard the team of agents come in behind him.

"Weird pattern for a bomb," one of them said as he took in the center of destruction.

"Rocket launcher through the front window." Alex pointed and began to sift through the chunks of charred plaster and furniture. "Sixty-six millimeter LAW."

"Right." The man followed his example. "Let's recover the bodies," he called out to the rest of the team.

Alex straightened and looked at him, as anger too strong to control welled up inside. His fist rose in the air. At the last second he turned and punched through a still-standing piece of drywall.

It didn't make him feel any better.

"Sorry. Didn't mean it like that." The agent drew back. "I— Did you know the…"

He nodded before the man could say victims. "Let's just see what we can find."

Within minutes the air was thick with dust from their work, the men coughing and spitting. Hard to see, too. He went through the mess methodically, one piece of broken furniture after the other, feeling more and more miserable with each second that ticked by. He shouldn't have left, although it might not have made a difference even if he'd been here. From the look of things, Nicola and Spike never stood a chance. The rocket launcher was probably shot from beyond the perimeter sensors. They had no warning. Alex worked like a madman while guilt and grief fought for the top spot inside him.

Twenty minutes passed before the call rang out from the corner by the back door.

"Man down."

Alex climbed over a chunk of kitchen cabinets and half a sofa, barely noticing the jagged piece of broken wood that scraped against his leg.

Spike.

Alex swallowed. His friend lay upside down on the basement stairs, probably knocked there by the explosion, buried in rubble up to his waist. He was still, too still, his face covered in white dust. Alex wouldn't allow himself to think he looked dead.

"Help me." He grabbed chunks of drywall and threw them to the side, then, once the task was mostly accomplished, moved up to Spike's head and left the rest for the agent to finish.

He brushed the dust off Spike's face and made sure his nostrils were free, then bent and set his head on the man's chest.

Nothing. No, wait. Something there. A faint heartbeat, so tentative he might have just imagined it. But then there it was again. Alex drew a shaky breath. "Still alive."

"Don't move him," came the response, as if he had to be told. "I'm getting the stretcher."

In another minute the team's medic was there.

"One, two, three." Alex assisted him in putting Spike on the stretcher and helped the man take his friend to the chopper.

The medic checked Spike's pupils then grabbed the IV kit. "I can handle it. Go find the other one."

Alex turned and ran for the house, hope filling him that there would be "another one" to find. If Spike had made it through the explosion somehow, then so could Nicola have. He hung on to that thought and refused to let go.

He tossed a broken side table out of the way and found the cage. It looked empty. Then he lifted it and heard the timid chirping from one of the nests. Miraculously, the Tweedles were fine. He ran the cage out to the chopper, surprised at how much the

Tweedles mattered. Despite their foul manners, the birds had grown on him.

The team searched for another hour, both inside and out, before they gave up. Nicola wasn't there. Even Alex had to accept that, when he found her necklace out front by the bushes. He ordered the team back to the helicopter. They had to get Spike to a hospital. The medic had stabilized him for now, but he clearly needed further treatment, more than they were able to provide.

"Better send over the cleanup crew," he told the Colonel on their way back. "Spike's unconscious but seems mostly whole. Nicola's gone." He took a deep breath. "I left a man at the house to keep it secure."

A moment of silence on the other end, then, "I'll tell the senator. I've got every free man we have working on possible U.S. connections for the Sons of Peace. Maybe we'll have something by the time you get back."

Alex looked down and unclenched his fists. He hoped they wouldn't be too late. He hoped she was still alive. He told himself it wouldn't have made sense for them to take her if she weren't.

But if she were still alive... He didn't want to think of the possibilities. If General Meng had taken her because he thought Barrington had betrayed him and he wanted to exact revenge on the senator, it meant he would want Nicola to suffer. Perhaps the same way his daughter had suffered.

The Colonel's words echoed in Alex's head about how the General's daughter had been raped and beaten by soldiers before taking her own life. Fear shot through him, fear and rage.

"Can't you make this damned thing go faster?" he yelled at the pilot, ready to pull him out of his seat and take over.

"We are going as fast as it'll go, sir."

Alex stared ahead, seeing nothing of the landscape they flew over. He had to get to Nicola in time.

NICOLA PACED THE FLOOR and fought the dread settling into her bones. Tomorrow would be a big day, the General had said, scaring her with that crazed look in his eyes. She didn't know his plans, but chances were, unless a miracle occurred, the upcoming day would be her last.

They had either kidnapped her to be a hostage to exchange for something they needed, in which case they'd find out soon the United States never negotiated. Or—she took a deep breath—they'd kill her in some graphic way to send whatever message it was they wanted her father to get.

Tired and cold and banged up pretty bad, she had no idea what to do next. Alex would know. God, she would have given anything to have his strong arms around her now. She didn't want to die without ever seeing him again.

She sank onto the floor in the corner. What were you supposed to do when you only had hours to live? She rested her head on her knees and prayed for a miracle.

''Nicola?'' Alex whispered in her ear, and she jumped at the sound of his voice.

His name tumbled from her lips before she realized he couldn't hear her.

''If you're receiving this, I want you to know that I'm coming to get you.''

The earpiece fell silent. *Don't stop talking. Please don't go away.*

''Hang in there, *querida,*'' he said after a while. ''And don't worry about anyone but yourself. We rescued Spike and the Tweedles. They'll be fine.''

He paused again.

''I'm sorry I left. I couldn't believe I allowed us to become personally involved. I didn't think I'd be the right person to protect you. I thought I'd be too distracted. Hell, I wasn't the right man for the job from the start. I couldn't see straight for wanting you.''

She wiped her eyes and wished she could talk to him, tell him where she was, tell him she didn't care about him leaving, only that he was back.

''You are going to get through this. You're as

tough as they come. Don't take any unnecessary chances. I'm going to find you and bring you home, then I'm going to cook you the biggest organic feast you've ever seen."

She couldn't help a small smile at that.

"I have to go now to work on figuring out where you are. Then I'm coming to get you. Count on it."

The earpiece went silent. She sat there for a while replaying in her head everything Alex had said, until the strength of his words filled her. She had no doubt he would come for her, but would he be too late? He only had until morning. Whatever the General was going to do to her, he had said it would be tomorrow. She would either have to get out of here and escape the General long enough for Alex to find her, or somehow let Alex know where she was so he could get here fast. If she could get to a phone, she could call the police.

But she could think of no way to break out of the room. Which meant she would have to think of a way to make them let her out. And hopefully soon. She hadn't gone to the bathroom since this morning. If they kept her locked in here much longer, she was going to embarrass herself.

Right. There's an idea. She got up and yelled through the window to the man who stood guard outside. "I have to go to the bathroom."

He ignored her.

"Please?"

The man yelled something across the yard, too fast, and in a dialect she didn't understand.

"I need to use the bathroom. Could you please let me out?"

He didn't so much as turn around.

She asked again and again, until she realized she was wasting her breath. The soldier was probably ordered to ignore her.

Great. Maybe this was part of the torture. Punishment because she'd tried to run away. Or perhaps it was their way of humiliating her. She paced the room, refusing to let them defeat her spirit. There had to be a way out of this. Alex would know. What was she missing? She replayed in her mind everything she'd seen and heard so far. Unfortunately, none of it gave her a brilliant idea to aid her escape.

She heard the scraping of a key in the lock and moved toward the door. Yes! Her plan worked. Once she was out of the basement, who knew what kind of opportunity would present itself? This might be her last chance. She was determined to take it.

She tried to look crestfallen and exhausted instead of pleased as the door opened. The barrel of a rifle entered the room first, then came a soldier who barely looked eighteen. He set a banged-up metal bucket on the floor then closed the door behind him.

What?

She had expected him to escort her out, up into the house. But he was gone so fast she hadn't had the chance to do anything. By the time she'd realized what he was doing, it was too late.

The door opened again and a small white ball blurred into the room. She ignored it to grab for the door. Her fingers closed around the knob, but by the time she threw her full weight into the pull, it was too late, the lock had already clicked.

Damn. She had hoped to be led to a bathroom, hopefully one with a window. She kicked the door, then turned around to look at what the guard had tossed in.

A crumpled wad of toilet paper.

How civilized.

Chapter Ten

Nicola sat on the floor in the far corner, and considered her options. She didn't have any. In the past two hours since the bucket had been brought in and then taken away, she'd had plenty of time to think of a new strategy but little success in coming up with a viable one.

General Meng had said he would send her some food. Hopefully soon. Not because she was hungry—she couldn't even think about eating—but because any time the door opened, it meant she might get a chance to do something. The best she came up with so far was to pretend to be listless when they brought the food in. She would make them think they had broken her resistance. Then when they came for her plate, she would use whatever utensils they would have given her to attack.

She tried to envision herself poking someone's eyes out with chopsticks. The image didn't quite gel, but she was desperate enough to give it a try if things came to that.

Boots scraped on the floor outside her door. Somebody was coming. She hung her head and sagged against the wall, watching from under hooded lids as a soldier came in and set a tray on the floor.

"Eat," the man said in Chinese. She looked up, making sure her gaze was confused and that she looked scared and unsure of what he wanted.

He pushed the tray toward her with the barrel of his rifle, then went to stand inside the door instead of leaving.

Was he going to watch her eat? Why? Did they want to make sure she kept her strength? For what?

Unease settled into her stomach, but she got up and dragged herself over to the food. She would eat to ensure she had the energy to fight.

They didn't give her chopsticks. She lifted the bamboo lid off a meal of fried rice and chicken and ate with her hands, forcing the food down her constricted throat into her stomach that was shrunken with tension. She wished she had something to wash the food down with, but they hadn't given her tea, either, no doubt not trusting her with scalding water. Too bad.

That left her the tray and the bamboo plate. Couldn't think of any way to use them as effective weapons against the man's gun. Maybe she could try the window again, after the soldier left. The guard outside couldn't possibly stay awake all night, could he? Maybe she could trick him somehow. She finished the meal, desperate for an idea. Before she could come up with anything, the young man took her tray. Instead of leaving, however, he passed it out the door and stayed with her.

Her panic rose, along with nausea. She shouldn't have forced the food down. Should have listened to her battered body's insistence that she was too nervous to eat.

She backed toward the corner, surprised when the floor swayed under her. Her head felt dizzy, her thoughts disoriented. She didn't think she was going to make it back to the wall. She sank to the floor and took a deep breath.

Then, with her last fully conscious thought, she figured it out. They had drugged her.

She was dimly aware of hands grabbing her, taking her clothes off. Somebody measured her then strapped something to her chest. Strapped it tight. She heard voices talking in Chinese. She recognized the General's voice but not the others, catching words at random as she slipped in and out of consciousness.

"...the U.S. will have to respond..."

"...bigger fiasco than they've ever seen before..."

"...first biological attack..."

"...our names..."

"...remembered in history..."

"...changed China..."

"...noble sacrifice..."

She had no idea how long she'd lain there before she began to come out of the drug-induced haze. The General squatted next to her, everyone else gone.

Her head was still swimming, her mouth dry, her thoughts disoriented. What had they done to her?

He patted her hand in a fatherly gesture. "I'm sorry about that, but it has been a necessary precaution. Couldn't allow you to thrash around while we were working, but now that it's secured, you're perfectly safe."

She looked down at her clothes, a white T-shirt and long blue pants. A work uniform? Her gaze settled on the plastic box strapped to her chest, the size of a dinner plate and about two inches thick.

"What is it?"

The General smiled, the emotion on his face a strange mixture of dementia and pride. "A bomb."

She was pretty sure she was going to lose consciousness again. Nicola held her breath, trying to keep the terror at bay. "Will it blow up if I move?"

"What would be point of that?"

What the hell was the point of strapping a bloody bomb to her? She wanted to scream but held herself in control. She took a slow breath and watched her chest rise, expecting the worst. The bomb didn't seem to mind her breathing. She sat up inch by inch, careful to avoid any sudden movement.

"You fine now. We only had to be careful while we put it together."

Right. Was that supposed to reassure her? "Why are you doing this?"

"For Chinese people, for what this country can give them."

So she was to be their hostage. That meant there would be negotiations. They would take her someplace where her father could see her, see the bomb. That had to be the whole point for her kidnapping. At least once she was there a SWAT team would be called in for sure, and Alex. Hope, sweet hope.

"Come, Nicola." The General stood and held his hand out to her. "Almost midnight. We better get on the road. Today we are the early crew."

She ignored his hand as she rose. Soldiers surrounded them as soon as they stepped through the door. They led her to a white van parked in the courtyard. The sign on the side advertised a cleaning service.

She glanced at the men who surrounded her, a dozen of them at least, all armed to the teeth. Her best bet was to go along and wait for the SWAT team.

''Your government very good to—how do you say—minority-owned businesses. Chinese-American man owns cleaning company for Capitol Hill.'' The General pushed her into the van. Seven soldiers followed. ''He too American to ask for help, but not smart. Brags too much about big contract and his best security. Today his workers went to work. Tonight they don't come home.''

As soon as the door closed behind them, the soldiers pulled blue cleaning uniforms, similar to hers, over their black army fatigues. The General followed their example after handing her a blue top to match her pants. She held it for a second. Where was the man it belonged to? Had the General's men killed the original cleaning crew when they'd taken the van?

The General watched her. ''Need help?''

She shook her head, then put on the garment with slow movements and sweating hands, not daring to take a full breath until she was done. The men settled in and fell silent. She watched through the small back window as the van sped through Chinatown, deserted in the middle of the night.

If they were to work on Capitol Hill, they must be in Washington. She would see her father, no doubt. She was pretty sure that had been the whole point to her kidnapping, to gain the attention of Senator Barrington.

What if she could reach the General somehow, if inside the fanatic there still existed a small remnant of the man she had once known? Maybe if she reminded him of those days when she had been a friend of his daughter's. "Where is Mei? I wrote to her, but she never responded."

The General's face darkened. He waited a long time before he spoke. "She is with her ancestors."

"She can't—" The stunned denial stumbled from her mouth as her brain struggled to process the news. Mei couldn't be dead. "How—"

The hatred that shot from the man's eyes made her draw back.

"She was betrayed." He looked away from her.

She wanted to know more but was afraid to ask. Had Mei's death made the General become the unrecognizable shadow of the man he had once been? Had the United States had something to do with it? Had her father? Was this some sort of revenge?

She looked at the bomb strapped to her chest. Dear God, what were they planning to do with her?

She fought her panic. She couldn't afford to become hysterical, to be distracted by fear. She had to keep her mind clear, had to keep focused. If the slightest chance presented itself for her to prevent the horrible violence that was to come, she had to take it.

She studied the men in the van. Six sat stoically,

while one—the young man who had brought her the bucket—kept fidgeting with his seat. If she were to break the chain, it was good to know where the weakest link was.

The General opened a hidden compartment in the floor and they exchanged their rifles for handguns that looked as if they were made of plastic. He tucked his under his uniform and out of sight, the rest of the men doing the same. ''Look like toy, but shoot well,'' he said.

She didn't doubt him.

They pulled into the parking lot without trouble, and before they got out, the General handed them their ID tags. He gave Nicola hers then pulled a small remote from his pocket.

''You smart girl. You got bomb, I got this.''

She nodded, understanding his message: Don't do anything or I'll blow your head off. She went to the service entrance with them, trying not to think about the fact that she was a walking explosive weapon.

They ran their access cards through the reader, then walked by the Capitol Hill Police officer on duty one by one. He only looked up from the monitors in front of him for a second to nod to them.

''You know what you need to do,'' the General said to his men once they were in the basement room that contained the cleaning supplies.

They each grabbed a cart and left.

"What now?" Nicola couldn't take her eyes off the man's right hand stuffed into his pocket, next to the remote.

"Now we wait." He rubbed his temple with his left.

"For what?"

"Joint Senate hearing at eight."

"And then?"

He smiled wickedly. "Then we, as you say in America, crash it."

THE RINGING PHONE woke Alex at two in the morning. His gaze slid from the clock to the towel-covered cage behind it on the nightstand. "Rodriguez." He sat up on the bed where he had slept fully dressed and lifted the towel, setting off an instant barrage of chirping. He couldn't believe he was now toting around two finches—in obvious need of anger-management counseling.

"We've got an address—184 Ming Street in Chinatown," Colonel Wilson said.

Alex was out of bed and throwing some food to the birds as he listened, then out the door, passing the soldier on guard at the army barracks where he had crashed the night before.

The Colonel went on. "Belongs to a prominent Chinese-American businessman who had some financial links to the Sons of Peace in the past. I already sent a team. You can meet them there.''

''On my way.'' He clicked off the phone as he reached his car. The guard opened the gate for him, and he peeled out of the base with the gas pedal touching the floor.

''Washington, D.C., 184 Ming Street,'' he said into the GPS and glanced at the map on the display. He knew the route and doubled the speed limit as he raced through deserted streets. Traffic was nonexistent at this hour of the night.

He parked one street back then ran for it, not slowing down until he could see the house, the largest building in the neighborhood. He stepped into the shadow of a deep doorway and scanned the area. Businesses slept under their metal window protections splattered with Chinese graffiti. A couple of stray cats inspected one of the garbage cans that lined the uneven sidewalk. He pulled back at the sound of an approaching car, but it passed by without slowing down and quickly disappeared from sight. No sign of the SWAT team. He looked back to the house. A place that big could hold an awful lot of surprises.

He flipped his phone open. ''I'm here. I'm going in.''

''I'll let the team know. They're only a few minutes behind you.'' The Colonel clicked off.

Alex clipped the phone on his belt and pulled out

his brand-new SIG-Sauer 9mm. He held the gun next to his leg as he walked toward the gate then past it, until he came to the end of the property where the stone wall met the next house. He glanced around, tucking the gun into his waistband. He grabbed a protruding rock above his head, pulled up, then heaved himself over the wall.

A garden. Dark. The streetlights didn't reach this far. He surveyed his surroundings while he listened. No sound in the night air gave him any clues or aroused his suspicions.

He kept an eye on the bushes and moved toward what seemed to be a courtyard ahead. He ran around the wall in a crouch and tried the first door he came to. Open. He didn't like it. He crept forward inch by inch and found himself in a long hallway. Still no sound. His entrance didn't set off any alarms.

He'd walked through the first few rooms in eerie silence when the sound of feet on gravel drew his attention. He stepped to the window, his back flat to the wall, and peered outside just in time to see the SWAT team fan out in the yard. If he had waited for them, they would have given him a radio for communications. As it was, he would have to make sure they didn't take him out by accident.

He caught the slightest sound of a door opening and walked out of the room to check the hallway. The door stood open—nobody was there. Then a shadow blocked the light as someone slipped through.

Alex stepped into plain sight and signaled to the man. The agent waited until his partner came in to cover his back, then walked over.

''Already checked all the rooms on the right of the hallway. They're empty. I'm going upstairs,'' he told the man.

The guy nodded and repeated the information into his radio for the rest of his team before moving toward the rooms on the left.

Alex crept up the staircase. Nobody in the upstairs hallway. His sense of foreboding grew. If Nicola were still there, the place would have been guarded. Unless, of course, it was a trap.

He tried the first door. An empty room. The second. Same.

Had Nicola been held here? If so, the rooms kept their secrets, all signs of occupants cleaned, the beds made.

He cleared three more rooms before he saw another member of the SWAT team coming up the stairs. The man had a radio for him. Alex fitted it into his ear, picking up short directions from the FBI agents on the property.

''Garden cleared.'' He heard a man say in a low voice.

''Garage cleared,'' said another.

"I've got something in the basement."

"Which way?" Alex spoke into his radio.

"Last door at the end of the hall as you come in the back."

He made his way swiftly through the house and found the right door within minutes. Two members of the SWAT team were already there, examining a small bare room.

"Looks like somebody took the window out." One of the men pointed.

He looked around the room, but other than the glassless window, could see nothing. Not even broken glass on the floor. Somebody had done a good job of cleaning up. "I'm going outside."

"Yes, sir."

He trotted up the stairs, not as careful about keeping silent as before. He was fairly sure they weren't going to find anyone here.

He spotted the window easily and crouched in front of it. Someone had done a thorough job of removing most of the glass.

"Anything there, sir?" one of the men asked from inside.

He looked at the pavers of the front yard, swept clean. Glass glistened in the cracks. "Not much." Looked like the window had been broken from the inside.

Had they kept Nicola in the basement? Had she

escaped? As much as he wanted to hold on to that glimmer of hope, the odds were overwhelmingly against it. If she had escaped, she would have gotten in touch with her father or the police by now.

But at the very least it looked as if she had *tried* to escape. The woman was a piece of work. Had to respect someone like that. She never gave up, did she? He hoped she could hang on a little longer. Come hell or high water, he was coming to get her.

"Sir, I found this in one of the garbage cans by the curb." An agent dragged a black plastic bag toward him and when he nodded, dumped the contents at his feet.

He recognized Nicola's shorts and tank top immediately. And then he caught sight of the bra. Soiled with blood.

The courtyard swam around him as cold rage filled his body until he thought he would explode with it. What had the bastards done to her?

He walked out into the garden where he had come in, and sank against the wall, leaving it to the agents to finish the search. He clipped his phone off his belt and set it to the right channel.

"Nicola?" What the hell could he say to her that would make any difference? What right did he have to tell her everything was going to be all right, with him standing here safe and sound while she—

He couldn't bear to think of it.

He'd kill them—anyone who had anything to do with this. Rage filled the gaping hole in his chest, the place from where his heart had gotten ripped out. Nicola was his heart, he realized with sudden clarity. And she was hurt because he had left her. That wasn't supposed to happen.

And he wasn't supposed to fall in love with her.

He had wanted her from the moment he'd first seen her, but during the last couple of days they'd spent together, the attraction had turned into something more with dizzying speed. He admired her courage, her compassion, her frankness. She could handle just about anything that came her way. He prayed she'd be able to handle this.

"Listen, *querida,* whatever they did to you, you're going to come through it. Hang on. I'm almost there." It looked as if they had only missed the General and his men by an hour or two, tops. He was close on their heels.

"No matter what they do, they can't touch your spirit. They can't change who you are, Nicola. You have to focus on that, what's inside. You are strong. Don't give up. I know it's hard, but I know you're brave. Just hang in there a little longer. It won't be long now."

And when he got there, he was going to shoot every one of those sons of bitches who had touched her. Then he would love her until she healed, plus another sixty to seventy years after that.

THE GENERAL LOOKED at Nicola's sleeping figure and for a moment he could see his daughter in her, the way things should have been. And for that split moment he wavered.

Chen followed his gaze. "Does she know?"

The General shook his head, his resolve back in place as strongly as ever. "I don't want her to struggle. It's better if she thinks there's a chance for her to walk away from this. I'll tell her what I'll tell the guard, that we have the bomb only to guarantee that we can get into the hearing and make our case for China."

Chen nodded. "And when we're in?"

"I push the button." And release the biological agent that would kill everyone in the room. Never had the U.S. seen a terrorist attack of that magnitude against high-level politicians. It would cripple the government. It would have to be responded to. American troops would be sent to China, the communist government toppled.

He would bring this about. This and more—the death of the man who had betrayed him and was responsible for what had happened to his wife and Mei. Today he would save his country and triumph over Barrington, his personal enemy.

He had waited for this day for a long time, had planned it in detail, between the endless periods of torture he'd suffered in prison. And now his time has come.

THE DOOR OPENED, and the sound startled Nicola. She hadn't even realized she'd fallen asleep. Alex had been talking to her on and off throughout the early morning. His voice was the only thing that kept her going, kept her from giving in to panic. His words had built an invisible shield that kept the outside world from getting to her. She could handle anything as long as she had that connection with Alex.

For the past couple of hours, she'd been forced to wait with the General for the rest of the "cleaning crew" to make their regular rounds. Everything had to look right on the security cameras.

One of the soldiers came in, parked his cart and reported on the position of security and the number of guards in the building, then left.

"Good." The General turned to Nicola. "I tell you what happens next so you won't make mistake. You very careful not to do that. Remember this?" He pulled the remote from his pocket.

How could she forget? Nicola nodded.

"We wait until the Senate hearing starts. Chen will spill five-gallon container cleaning liquid in front of the door. We walk by and stop to help clean up. One guard stands at the door. We use you to get in.''

''They'll never let you into a roomful of senators, even if you had a hundred hostages. The U.S. doesn't negotiate.''

If she had hoped to talk sense into him, she had failed. He went on as if he hadn't heard her.

''If he gives us trouble we shoot him. Not first choice. Shooting will bring many security too soon. When we are inside the room, rest of my men move into place and make sure nobody comes in until we finish.'' The General looked at his watch. ''In few minutes the Sons of Peace will be China's newest heroes. Your name on the morning news all over the country. Neither of us ever forgotten.''

Goose bumps covered Nicola's arms at the man's words. A mad light shone in his eyes, his conviction fueled by insanity. Despite the fact that he held her life, literally, in his hand, she could not hate the man, only pity him.

They waited another twenty minutes before the time came to go. The General grabbed a cleaning cart and pushed another toward Nicola. ''Take it.''

She did so without argument, eyeing the mop.

He exited the room as if he had every right to be where he was and walked down the hall with the push cart as if he'd done it every day of his life. She followed, keeping her eyes open for any opportunity.

Might not be many of those, if any at all. They were getting close to the grand finale. She passed a conference room and caught their reflection mirrored in the glass—two ordinary custodians in identical uniforms, plodding down the hall in no particular hurry.

She made a point of paying attention to every door, every exit sign as they passed. She looked at each security camera as they got to it. Keeping her hands on the cart, she stuck out her thumb and index finger making the sign of a gun. Couldn't do more than that with the General a few feet ahead of her, but she hoped the gesture would catch someone's eye.

"COLONEL SAYS you had a busy night," Thompson joked over the phone. He had joined the SDDU right when it started, at the same time as Alex, so they'd gotten to know each other during the initial training.

"Busy but unproductive." Alex skimmed through the reports he had gotten from Sylvia, a folder full of intelligence on the Sons of Peace. They were an odd lot with a single common denominator—none of them had anything to lose. "What's up? Anything new on the Hill?"

"Not sure. I've been going through the security tapes this morning, checking up on the overnight footage just in case. It appears someone fitting Nicola Barrington's description entered the Capitol Building at 12:38 with the cleaning crew. Hard to tell, the security video is pretty grainy. I had Senator Barrington view it. He's ninety percent sure it's his daughter.''

Alex tossed the reports on the desk as adrenaline shot through his body. ''Only ninety?''

''He hasn't seen her in the last couple of years.''

Busy man. He'd sacrificed an awful lot for his country— Then the pieces fell into place all of a sudden, and it all made sense.

''I'm on my way.'' He grabbed his bag of tricks and headed out the door. He had come back to his temporary room on the army base to go over the paperwork Sylvia had given him, and to maybe catch a brief nap. When action broke, he wanted to be fully functional and ready. ''Does the Colonel know?''

''Yeah. Called him first but he was over at the DHS in a meeting with the Homeland Security Secretary. Those two spend more time together than honeymooners. Something big is going down somewhere.''

''There's always something big going down somewhere in the world.'' But at the moment he wished no part of it. All he wanted was Nicola safe. His instincts said they had something bigger than a simple kidnapping. Bigger even than whatever international operation the Secretary and the Colonel were working on. ''What did the Colonel say?''

‘‘Not enough of us to go around. He’s calling in the FBI. I already put the Capitol Hill Police on alert.’’

‘‘Where is the senator?’’

‘‘He just left for a joint hearing. He’s got his security detail with him. I’m about to go over there myself.’’

‘‘Get him to a secure location immediately. Seal the building, double security. I’ll be there in fifteen minutes. If you see the woman on the security cameras, keep track of where she is but do not approach her or anyone with her until I get there.’’

‘‘You think this is it?’’

‘‘Yeah, and it’s going to be worse than we expected. If all General Meng wanted was to take out Senator Barrington and his daughter, he could have killed the daughter by now and gone after Barrington in his car or in his home. The senator has good security, but not nearly as good as the Capitol does.’’

‘‘They want the whole Congress,’’ Thompson said in a stunned voice.

‘‘Or as many senators and representatives as they can get. Meng is not just avenging his family. That’s just the icing on the cake. He’s planning a major terrorist attack on the U.S. government.’’

‘‘Oh, hell.’’

‘‘Make sure you clear whatever room Barrington was supposed to be in this morning.’’

He ended the call and dialed the Colonel next to update him on the developing situation. They were going to need a lot more than the FBI. He wanted the National Guard and the capital area National Emergency Response Team. Plus the Marine Corp's Chemical Biological Incident Response Force on standby, just in case.

He drove like a madman, planning as he went. He'd been an idiot to think that caring for Nicola would make him weaker. Hell, loving her was what gave him strength. He'd take the Capitol apart stone by stone to get to her.

NICOLA WATCHED a CHP officer walk down the hall toward them. She held her breath. Had he seen her on the video? She tried to catch his eye, but the man walked on without looking at them. She turned, unable to believe he would stroll by without giving her a chance to do something to grab his attention.

He stopped and put his finger to his headset, then looked at them, straight at Nicola as he said something into the mouthpiece. She was too far to hear his words, but the intent look in his eyes gave her hope.

She nodded her head slightly. The man turned and continued on his way without giving her any sign of having seen it.

So much for that. He'd probably been just staring

off into space while listening to whoever was talking into his ear. She'd had an opportunity and missed it, had no idea what to do with it. What if she had lifted her top so he could see the bomb? Could she have done it without the General noticing? She needed a plan so when they came across the next person, she would be ready.

The opportunity came faster than she had expected. They came to the end of the hallway, to a door flanked by two officers. Chen was on his knees in front of them, cleaning up a neon-green puddle.

The General stopped.

She looked at the officers, trying to warn them, trying to think of something to do or say that would give them a chance, to save them somehow without having the General blow her up. Her hands shook, her mind frozen with fear.

The General pulled his gun and in one smooth motion had it at her temple. "I want to go in," he said, his voice as calm and friendly as if he had brought lunch for them instead of death and destruction.

The officers drew their weapons simultaneously and so did Chen.

"Daughter of Senator Barrington." The General poked her with his gun. "I want little time. Thirty minutes to make case for my country. Nobody gets hurt."

"Drop your weapons." One of the officers stepped closer.

The General shook his head. "We go in or Miss Barrington dies."

Maybe she should tell them they had a bomb. She glanced at the General, his left hand in his pocket. Would he blow the bomb right here?

The second officer was moving toward Chen. *Second* officer. Nicola stared him. When General Meng's man had come into the cleaning room a while ago he had said there was *one* man in front of the room. Since then, someone had doubled the guard. Why? Were they expecting them? Had they set a trap?

"I will count to five," the General said. "If you don't move from door, I shoot."

The officers glanced at each other.

The General smiled. "One, two, three, four, f—"

The younger man stepped out of the way and shoved the door open.

It was easy, too easy, she thought, but then her heart sank at the sight inside. No SWAT team, no special commando, just a roomful of men and women in the middle of a Senate hearing.

Nobody noticed their entry, the room's attention focused on the speaker at the front. Since they came in at the back, most of the thirty or so senators sat with their backs to them.

The General pulled the remote from his pocket and flicked a switch, and she squeezed her eyes shut, expecting to be dead the next moment.

She heard him speak instead. ''I armed the bomb now. When I lift my finger from this button it blows.''

She was hyperventilating as she opened her eyes and prayed the man didn't have twitchy fingers. She hadn't thought things could get worse than having a bomb strapped to her chest with the remote in a madman's hand, but she had underestimated the General. Now that he had activated the pressure trigger, her fate was sealed. If the man succeeded and blew the bomb she would die. If Secret Service had set some kind of trap and managed to take him out, when he let go of the remote, she would die...with too many things left unsaid. She searched the room for her father.

''Ladies and gentlemen.'' The General spoke loud enough for his voice to carry in the room.

A couple of people turned in their direction. Some gasped at the sight of her with a gun to her head. More senators looked, some came out of their chairs. The General pushed her forward, keeping the gun steady at her temple. She tried not to give him the satisfaction of seeing her tremble but failed miserably.

''No panic, please.'' He walked to the front of the

room with her. ''Take your seats. Agenda changed today. We talk about People's Republic of China. Very neglected.''

He scanned the room. ''Senator Barrington, you remember your old friend?''

Nicola looked from face to face, none of them familiar. Her father wasn't there, her only relief in all of this. The General had miscalculated. At least, her father would live.

The General waited. ''You remember your daughter, then?'' He shoved Nicola forward.

''Senator Barrington was called out earlier,'' someone in the back said.

''He has ten minutes to return.'' Fury flooded the General's face as he turned toward the security camera in the corner closest to them and reached over to rip open Nicola's uniform top to expose the bomb. ''If he wants to see his daughter alive.''

Chapter Eleven

The next second, two dozen weapons were trained on them as the ''senators'' knocked the tables on their sides and took cover behind them, their guns pointed at the General and Chen.

So someone had known they were coming and they had set a trap. Nicola was grateful, even though it probably wouldn't change much for her. But at least her father and the other senators who were supposed to be in this morning's hearing were safe.

''I want to talk to Senator Barrington,'' the General shouted. ''I want to make case for China. Don't want to hurt anybody.''

Nicola looked at the men who had the General cornered. They were eyeing the bomb, considering how much damage it could really do, no doubt. She knew next to nothing about explosives but it hardly seemed big enough to take out a room this size.

Then words she had overheard the night before

came back to her, *first biological attack.* Her heart stopped when she finally understood. The small bomb on her chest was a biological weapon. The explosion might not bring down the building, but it would be enough to get the biological agents into the air and take out a good chunk of the United States Senate, had they been in the room.

And it might do the job yet. Once the bomb blew and the biological agents got into the Capitol's ventilation system, who knew how many people would be affected before the building was evacuated?

She looked from one officer to the next as they kneeled behind the tables—men and women. They were putting their lives at risk to save her father and his colleagues. To save her. And they were all going to die.

None of them realized the General had a biological weapon, and even if she shouted her newfound knowledge, nobody was close enough to stop the man before he got a chance to blow the bomb.

Except her.

When Alex had risked his life to save hers, she hadn't been able to comprehend it, but now she did. Faced with a group of individuals whose lives depended on her, she finally understood Alex and found the answer to the question she had so often asked in the past—how much a private citizen owed her country.

Everything.

She had heard of World War II soldiers throwing themselves onto hand grenades to save their comrades. Could she do the same? Would it be enough?

Maybe it was a day for miracles and she could gain control of the remote from the General. If she managed that, she was pretty sure he'd be taken out before he could manage to squeeze off a shot at her. She could make it out of this room alive.

And if her plan didn't work, at the very least, if she threw herself on him facedown, the bomb would be between their bodies and that might cushion the blow. It could give the people present enough time to get out of the room before the biological agents dispersed in the air. Maybe she could gain them enough time for someone to shut down the ventilation system. That was key. Otherwise the lives of hundreds of people would be jeopardized.

Too many maybes, but what was the alternative? She couldn't let them all die. If she failed, they still wouldn't be any worse off than if she hadn't tried at all. She had nothing to lose.

The risk was high. If she failed she would pay the ultimate price. But for a chance to save countless lives, it was a risk she was willing to take.

She understood Alex completely then, and for that moment the connection between them seemed stronger than ever.

All morning she had hoped he would get there to rescue her before something horrible happened. Now she was glad she didn't see him among the people in the room. She hoped he would get there too late. For once maybe she would be able to save him.

She said a prayer. Took a deep breath. She wished she could have talked to her father and Alex one last time. She hoped they would understand why she did what she was about to do.

The General was shouting at the security camera, enraged, getting more and more agitated. She had no time to lose.

Nicola lunged at the General and yelled, "Biological weapon," as she knocked him to the ground. They rolled on the blue carpet as he fought her, not letting go of the remote. He was still waiting for her father.

But instead of running for safety, the officers were right there, and so was Alex. He jumped on the General and grabbed the hand that held the remote, putting his thumb on top of the General's, going for the other hand at the same time to hold off the gun.

"Move back, Nicola," Alex ordered without looking at her as he struggled with the General, trying to control the man.

Not a chance. She grabbed the plastic gun and wrested it from the General's hand that Alex held by the wrist. She wanted to help more, but a couple of officers pulled her away while others took her place.

"Barrington!" the General howled as his muscles bunched and he heaved to pull his hand from Alex's grip. He looked at Nicola, madness clouding his eyes. "We will be remembered."

His thumb was still on the remote under Alex's and he thrashed in an attempt to gain control. Then there were too many officers around them, and Nicola could barely see, until Alex straightened.

He had the remote in his hand.

"You okay?" He walked to her, leaving the General to the Capitol Hill Police.

He pulled her into a tight embrace with his free hand, and she sagged against the safety of his broad chest, unable to speak. From the corner of her eyes, she saw Chen led out of the room and the bomb squad come in. They headed straight for her.

"Everybody step back." A short man in protective gear said to the agents as he reached Nicola. He was Chinese.

She cringed against Alex, as she stared at the man's face, trying to remember if he was one of the General's men.

"Relax," he said in a sympathetic voice. "I'm one of the good guys."

"And lucky for you, Jim is one of the best." Another man in a protective suit came to look at the bomb.

"Sorry." She held the torn uniform aside to allow them a better look.

"Not a problem," Jim said. "I can understand why you'd be a little jumpy."

The other guy got down on his knees in front of her and gently touched the straps. "You said biological?"

She nodded and hoped he would say, No problem, we disarm things like that every day.

Instead he stepped back. "Do you know the range of the remote?"

"No." The General hadn't said anything about that.

"Should be good for at least a couple of feet. You need to move back and put on protective gear, sir," Jim said to Alex.

"I'm staying where I am." He grabbed her hand and held it tight.

"You have to—"

"I don't have to do anything." Alex's voice was as rigid as steel.

"Yes, sir. We'll start as soon as this wing of the building is evacuated."

The CHP had already removed the General, and the few remaining officers were on their way out.

Three other men came through the door in white overalls, gas masks hanging around their necks.

Jim walked over to them.

"Who are they?" Nicola asked Alex.

"CBI Response Force," he said, then when she threw him a questioning look, explained. "Chemical Biological Incident team. Marine Corps. They'll take over the bomb once it's disarmed."

She began to shake, uncontrollably so. "I'm cold."

"You're in shock. Sit down." Alex pulled over a chair for her, then another for himself so he could sit next to her and hold her.

"I really thought this was it for me."

"Nothing is going to happen to you as long as I live and breathe." He tightened his arms around her and held her close until Jim came back with two gas masks for them. Alex helped her before he slipped on his.

She looked around and watched people leave, until only the bomb squad and Alex and she remained. Alex squeezed her hand and she leaned her head against him, soaking up his solid strength for as long as she dared. Then she closed her eyes and pulled away. "You should move back and put on protective gear." Her voice sounded funny coming through the gas mask.

She felt his warm hand back on hers the next second. She opened her eyes and turned to look at him. "I mean it." She tried to shrug him off, but he wouldn't let go.

"I'm not going anywhere, *querida.*"

Jim knelt in front of her. "Let's get started then. Try to stay as still as possible."

She turned her head from the man and buried it against Alex's shoulder. No way could she watch.

Alex put his chin on the top of her head. "Don't worry. These guys know what they're doing."

God, she hoped so. "How's my father?"

"Worried about you. One of the men on his security team spotted you coming in this morning so we had him safely tucked away. I only wish I could have gotten to you sooner."

"You got to me. That's all that counts." She lifted her head to look at him.

"Did they hurt you?" His dark gaze, full of emotion, burned into hers.

"No." She watched him release his breath.

"I thought... Since Meng Mei..."

"What happened to her?"

She listened, tears rolling down her face as he told her the story. Mei had been like a sister to her. Her tragic fate shook Nicola. What kind of world did they live in where something like that could happen?

"You're a strange woman, you know." Alex watched her. "Stand up fine to kidnapping and nearly getting blown up, but you cry at the news that the daughter of the man who wanted to kill you died."

"She was my friend."

Jim tugged at the straps. "I think we're okay. I got the trigger mechanism disabled. You may release the remote."

"You sure?" Alex pinned the man with a stare.

"Yes, sir."

He hugged her tight, and Nicola held her breath as she watched him lift his thumb, millimeter by millimeter.

Nothing happened.

She took a shaky breath as Alex handed the remote to one of the men on the squad.

He pulled off his gas mask. "It's over, *querida.*"

She nodded and followed his example, then held up her arms while he helped the men get the contraption off her.

Then they were standing and he pulled her to him, his strong arms wrapped around her like a protective cocoon.

"Alex." She couldn't do more than whisper his name into the crook of his neck, her knees going weak from relief.

He scooped her up in his arms and walked out of the room with her, his forehead resting against hers. "I wanted to tell you we were in the building, but I was afraid they might have gotten the earpiece from you and were listening.''

''I still have it. I heard everything you said before. It helped, Alex. Thank you.''

His eyes narrowed as his sensual lips pulled into a smile on their way down to claim her mouth. He stopped walking as he focused all his attention on kissing her senseless, and she melted into his warmth, into the security of his arms.

The world disappeared from around them as she lost all awareness except for the feel of his lips on hers, his tongue that claimed her and sent pleasure coursing through her body.

''Hate to interrupt, but...''

They pulled apart at the words and she stared at the imposing figure of a black man who stood in front of them. When had he gotten there?

''Colonel.'' Alex nodded to the man but didn't release her.

The Colonel looked as if he was struggling with a grin. ''I believe there are a couple of medics and an ambulance outside, waiting to check out Miss Barrington. Nobody is allowed to enter the building until the FBI and CHP clear it. Maybe you could escort the young lady out.''

''Will do.'' Alex hesitated for a moment. ''About that recovery leave you said a while back I should be taking...''

"Yes?"

"This would be a good time. A couple of days maybe."

The man lifted an eyebrow and looked at Alex for a few moments. "I see." He turned to Nicola. "That was a brave thing you did in there, distracting the man long enough so CHP could take him down. Your father ought to be proud of you."

"How is he?"

"Shaken with worry. We had to physically restrain him from coming to see you. But the building is not one hundred percent secure yet, although we're working on it."

She nodded.

"Get our heroine to the ambulance then clean up this mess, Rodriguez." The Colonel clapped Alex on the shoulder, then walked away.

"How is your arm?" Nicola asked as Alex began moving down the hall.

"Fine. How about you? Are you okay?"

"You asked for a recovery leave—"

"I was hoping to spend it with you."

"Oh." Happiness filled her at his words.

A couple of days with Alex were more than what she had dared hope for. She understood now why the country needed men like him out there, why it needed people like her father.

Alex obviously cared for her. That would have to

be enough. Anything more, like a shared future, would be impossible. She could never be so selfish as to ask him to give up his job. A couple of days with him sounded like heaven. She was grinning like an idiot as Alex deposited her in the ambulance that waited out front.

"How is Spike doing?" She remembered suddenly, and felt bad for not asking sooner.

"He's over at the military hospital. Both legs broken, a couple of busted ribs, some missing skin." Alex looked grim. "Both of his eardrums were blown out."

"Can I visit him?"

"I'll take you over later." He glanced toward the small army that surrounded the building.

"You should go see if you can help get things wrapped up," she said. "Be careful."

"Excuse us for a second," he said to the paramedics as he stepped between them and pulled her into his arms, the blood pressure cuff dangling by her side. He kissed her so gently, it nearly made her cry.

Then before he left, he ordered the two young men to take her to the hospital for a full checkup.

She watched him run up the stairs on his way to finish saving the world. She loved his dedication and the knowledge that he would come and find her when he was done. She pretty much loved everything about him. No matter how hard she had tried to avoid it, she had fallen in love with the man.

NICOLA CAME OUT of the shower and rubbed her hair with the plush towel the maid had set out. She had decided to stay in Washington for the night, at her father's insistence. She wasn't ready to return to Devon and deal with her smoke-damaged house.

Someone knocked on the door. The maid had already left for the day, and she wasn't expecting Alex for another hour. He had called several times. Stuck in meetings with the Colonel, he'd said. Couldn't tell her more than that. He'd promised to take her over to the military hospital to see Spike in a little while.

"Nicola?" her father's voice came through the door.

"Come in, Dad." She tightened the belt of her robe and tossed the wet towel on the back of a chair.

"Are you okay?" He walked into her room hesitantly. "Should I come back later?"

"It's fine. I'm fine," she said.

He ran his fingers through his graying hair. When had he gotten old? He'd lost weight, as well, she noticed, ashamed that she hadn't visited him for so long.

"I'm so sorry about what happened." He searched her face.

"It wasn't your fault. You can't control every maniac out there."

He nodded, his face somber. "I'm sorry about everything before this, too."

She blinked away the tears that threatened to fill her eyes.

"After—" he took a deep breath and went on "—after your mother died…I couldn't cope with it. I blamed myself. I threw myself into work. I didn't know how to raise you, so I focused on what I did know. I wanted a bill for more money for cancer research. I wanted to fight against the disease that took your mother."

He'd done that and more. She looked at him, seeing him anew.

"I was obsessed with fear of losing you, too. I was on every committee that had to do with crime or drugs, anything I thought might threaten your future. I wanted to protect you." His eyes glistened. "I know I went about it all wrong."

"All I ever wanted was your love. A little attention," she said, her throat burning with unshed tears.

"You have that. You always had it." He came to her to hug her, and kissed the top of her head as he used to do when she was a child. "I want to change things between us. I don't want to waste another day."

"Me, too, Dad," she choked out, hugging him back.

The past few days had changed everything for her. In a way she felt as if she'd never really grown up until now. After being in so much danger, her life and the people she loved seemed infinitely more precious. She understood her father more—what he did for this country. And for the first time, she appreciated the sacrifice.

"I love you, Dad." She rested her head on the wide chest against which she had so often been comforted as a child.

"I love you, too," he whispered.

NICOLA TURNED OFF the hair dryer and listened. There it was again. Somebody was knocking on her door. She walked out of the bathroom. Had her father forgotten something?

"Come in, Dad."

"He went for a walk." Alex stood in the doorway, wearing a tailored suit and a dizzying smile.

She had to catch her breath before she could talk. "I wouldn't have thought you owned one of these."

"Bought it this morning. Got nervous about going to court a senator's daughter. May I come in?"

She stepped aside, feeling as giggly as a teenager. "I heard that a good shopping spree is just the thing to relax you after a day of armed confrontation."

His grin widened. ''Hardly a spree. I only bought three things.''

''What are the other two?''

He walked out to the hallway and brought in a cage, covered with a towel.

''Is that...'' She pulled the towel off, tears springing to her eyes to see her Tweedles safe and sound. He'd said he'd bought two more things. She'd expected a pair of new birds. The Tweedles were quiet for once, picking at something shiny hanging on a silk cord from the top of the cage.

Alex pulled up the cord, and held out a key.

''I put a down payment on a house in Cleveland Park this morning. It has a huge sunroom with two overgrown banana trees. I thought maybe the Tweedles would like it.''

''A house?''

''I'd like you to stay there until your place gets fixed.'' He held her gaze. ''Or forever.''

Forever? Her heart screamed *yes!* but for the life of her she couldn't get anything intelligent past her lips.

Alex went on. ''I got two days from the Colonel. After that I'll have to leave on a mission. But when I come back, I'll be taking over training for a while, here in Washington.''

''Is that what you want?'' She didn't want him to give up doing what he loved for her.

"A bunch of rookies engaged in live ammunition exercises should keep me in enough excitement." He grinned. "I hope to see some action at home, as well." Then he grew serious. "I want to work in a job that makes a difference. If it ever comes to that, I will gladly give my life for my country. But right now the Colonel needs a good training officer as much as he needs me out there. And as important as this country is to me, so are you."

He pulled a blue velvet box from his pocket and got down on one knee. "I love you, Nicola Barrington. Will you marry me?"

She clutched her chest, struck speechless again.

"I know it's kind of sudden. You haven't known me for long. But I want you to think about it. Maybe you can give me your answer when I come back. I know you're the only woman for me and—"

"It is," she said finally, unable to do anything but echo his words, "kind of sudden."

"I'm a soldier. Once I decide on a course of action, I execute without hesitation."

She swallowed.

"Plus I figured you might still be worn-out from your experience and I had a better chance of knocking down your defenses in your weakened state."

"Lord, Alex. I never had any defenses when it came to you. I love you." She threw herself into his arms, knocking him to the floor.

His wide chest felt solid beneath her, his heart beating strong and steady. He gathered her close and kicked the door shut.

His deep voice sent delicious shivers through her when he spoke. "I don't ever want to let you go."

And she was glad. Because nowhere on earth would she ever feel as right as in the circle of his arms. She nuzzled his neck, then pressed her lips to his warm skin and drank in his familiar scent. She belonged with him. They belonged together. She had no doubts about that.

He kissed her hair, and when she lifted her head, he brushed his lips against hers, gently at first then more possessively. She gasped as he cupped her breast, awakening her body. "Should we move to the bed?"

The grin he shot her lit up his handsome face. "Hey, who is in charge of this operation?" He thumbed her nipple, sending a wave of pleasure through her.

She slid a hand between them and showed him.

Epilogue

Nicola stretched as she drank in the breathtaking view, the gently rolling water of the bay, brilliant blue tinted with orange, reflecting the sky above. The hillside lay like an emerald carpet below them. She could see their balcony at the Hawaiian Hilton from here, and it brought back memories of the night before.

"You were right." Alex finished his Tai Chi and came up behind her to sneak his hands around her waist and share the beauty of the sunrise.

She loved the way he couldn't seem to keep from reaching for her anytime they were near each other. Happiness greater than she had ever thought could exist filled her, and she turned in his arms for a kiss.

"Mmm…" She pulled away when his hands slid under her tank top. "We should probably go and say goodbye to our guests."

"Come to think of it—" He took her hand as they

walked down the hillside. ''The sooner our wedding guests leave, the sooner we can get started with our honeymoon.''

''And we'll be right in the hotel, with that lovely suite waiting.'' Nicola picked up the pace, liking the way the man's brain worked.

Alex grinned, then stopped. ''On the other hand, we're already here.''

''Here?'' She glanced around. The meadow looked like something straight out of a dream, hibiscus blooming everywhere, palm trees providing a canopy above and soft grass at their feet. ''What if someone sees us?''

''Nobody gets up this early in the morning unless they're chirped out of bed by bickering finches. The Tweedles are going home with the guests.''

She smiled. They had been too busy the night before to remember to cover the cage. And once the birds woke them this morning, she had talked Alex—with wicked promises—into some Tai Chi on the top of the hill, combined with watching the sunrise. She hadn't considered that he would want those promises fulfilled so soon.

He sat and pulled her down to the grass next to him. ''I promise you it's perfectly safe. I don't think this island has ever been this safe, nor will it likely be again.''

He was right about that. A number of Alex's teammates had shown up for the wedding, along with Colonel Wilson. Spike had the honor of being the best man, with both legs in casts.

"What if my father is looking for me?"

"The morning after your wedding night?" He lay back on the grass and pulled her with him.

"It seems he's always looking for me lately."

"Trying to make up for lost time, that's all. I think he finally realized what he missed."

"Maybe he—"

Alex silenced her with a kiss, then pulled back. "Nicola, I don't want to talk about your father."

He was right. Neither did she. Now that he was half on top of her, his palm covering her breast, she didn't want to talk at all. There were much more important things to be taken care of.

She pulled his head down for another kiss. And, being the take-charge type of man he was, he took it from there.

* * * * *

In January 2005, watch for
SECRET SOLDIER by Dana Marton.
Passion and peril collide on a faraway
land when Spike heads up his own
high-stake SDDU mission!

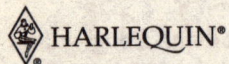

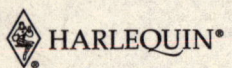

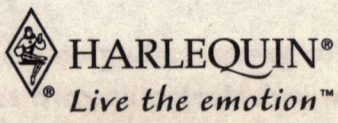